"You want to know how I feel? I feel like kissing you," Declan growled

And before Rachel could protest that they barely knew each other, that they were in a public place, that he was supposed to be protecting her, not kissing her, his mouth came down on hers. And she forgot everything else.

Her knees turned to jelly and she clutched his shirt in her hands just to remain upright. She hadn't kissed a man in a long time, but still, she hadn't remembered it being quite so wonderful. So intoxicating.

As he kissed her, his hands wandered over her body, skimming along her spine, smoothing across her hips. The light cotton fabric of her dress was thin enough that she could feel the heat of his palms. And when he bent to touch the bare skin of her thigh, a tiny moan escaped her throat and he suddenly stopped.

Declan stepped away from her. "I shouldn't have done that. You're a client."

Rachel frowned, then shook her head. "No. My boss, Trevor Ross, is your client. He's the one paying you, right?"

"That's good enough for me," Declan murmured just before taking her m~~~~~~~~~~~~~ kiss.

Blaze™

Dear Reader,

What could be better than two sexy Irish-American heroes? How about three? My Quinn trilogy comes to an end this month with the third brother, Declan. And with an even ten Quinn books behind me, you'd think I'd be finished, right? Not quite.

In this last book of the trilogy, Declan Quinn, security expert, meets a woman who professes an expertise in something completely different—sex. Radio sex-therapist Rachel Merrill is in need of protection, the kind of protection only Declan can provide. But as Dec gets to know Rachel, he learns that experimentation is always more interesting than research theories.

The Quinn family saga wraps up in January with *The Legacy*, the story of Emma Callahan Quinn's ancestors. In this book you'll meet the indomitable Jane Byrne, who, along with her infant daughter, survives the famine in Ireland to inspire generations of her female descendants. I enjoy hearing from my readers, so be sure to visit my Web site at www.katehoffmann.com.

Happy reading,

Kate Hoffmann

KATE HOFFMANN
The Mighty Quinns: Declan

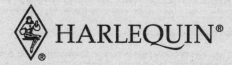

HARLEQUIN®

TORONTO • NEW YORK • LONDON
AMSTERDAM • PARIS • SYDNEY • HAMBURG
STOCKHOLM • ATHENS • TOKYO • MILAN • MADRID
PRAGUE • WARSAW • BUDAPEST • AUCKLAND

ISBN-13: 978-0-373-79295-5
ISBN-10:   0-373-79295-6

THE MIGHTY QUINNS: DECLAN

www.eHarlequin.com

Printed in U.S.A.

ABOUT THE AUTHOR

The Mighty Quinns: Declan is Kate Hoffmann's fiftieth story for Harlequin Books. Her first book was published in 1993, and since then she has enjoyed creating sexy heroes that her heroines (and her readers) can't possibly resist. Kate lives in a small town in Wisconsin with her three cats and her computer. She enjoys golfing, genealogy and gardening and also volunteers with music and theater programs for young people in her community. Her favorite place in the whole wide world is her bedroom. But her second-favorite place is Ireland, and it was there that the fairies worked their magic and put the Mighty Quinns in her path.

Books by Kate Hoffmann

Prologue

"LEMME SEE!"

Declan Quinn held tight to the high stone wall as his big brother Ian gave him a shove. His grandmother's opera glasses were clutched in his left hand as he trained them on the girl below. She was dressed only in a bikini, red with little yellow flowers. Lying on her stomach on a beach towel, she'd undone her top, and from the right angle, Dec could almost see her breast.

"Give me the damn binoculars," Ian whispered.

With a low curse, Declan handed Ian his grandmother's opera glasses, then swung his leg over the wall and straddled it. Kitty Donahue was fifteen years old and the daughter of their grandmother's gardener. She usually accompanied her father on his Saturday chores. During the winter months, she sat in the solarium and worked on her studies. But in the summer, Dec and his brothers were treated to the mysteries of the female body as she sunbathed in a quiet corner of the garden.

She reached back to brush a bug from her shoulder and Ian moaned softly. "I can almost see it."

"See what?"

They both looked down to find their little brother,

Marcus, standing below them, a frown creasing his brow. "Nothing," Dec said. "Go away, Marky."

"What are you lookin' at?" Marcus asked. He grabbed the tree that grew beside the wall and scrambled up on the other side of Dec. Searching through the bower of leaves, he finally spied the object of their interest and grinned. "She's almost naked!" he cried.

"Shhhh!" Dec clamped a hand over Marcus's mouth. "If you're going to be up here, you have to be quiet."

Wide-eyed, Marcus nodded and Dec slowly removed his hand. He took the opera glasses back from Ian and continued his study of Kitty. She was just about the most beautiful girl he'd ever seen—besides his mother and his sisters, Mary Grace and Jane.

He tipped his head back and closed his eyes, trying to picture them in his mind. It had been five years that June since he and his brothers had been home, five years since they'd last seen their parents or their older siblings. There were times when Dec wondered if they'd ever be reunited, or if the three youngest Quinn brothers would spend their entire lives in Ireland, living with their Grandmother Callahan.

Life with their maternal grandmother had been rough at first. Grace Callahan had never been a part of her grandchildren's lives, living an ocean away in Ireland, estranged from her daughter, Emma. Though it had never been made clear to the boys, some disagreement had caused their mother to stop speaking to their grandmother long before they were born.

Still, every summer there had been an invitation for the Quinn children to visit Ireland. It was only after Emma

Quinn had become horribly sick with cancer that she had finally allowed any of her children to go. And then, she'd sent just the youngest three, keeping the older children back to help support the family in the midst of mounting medical bills.

There had been no health insurance, no savings in case of emergency, but that hadn't stopped Paddy Quinn from searching out the finest medical care for his wife. He and the older children worked at any job they could find, with little left over for luxuries like decent food, new clothes—or a visit to Ireland.

It was Ian who had taken over the role of father figure to the younger boys, appointing himself the boss of everything. Dec didn't mind. Someone had to watch over them and though Dec was qualified, he had better things to spend his time on—like thinking about Kitty Donahue and all the other pretty Irish lasses who caught his fancy. Kitty was mysterious and fascinating and exciting. And she barely knew he existed.

"I can almost see her titties," Marcus whispered.

Ian gave him a sharp elbow to the ribs. "Where did you learn that word?"

"Listenin' to you tossers," Marcus said. "Besides, that's what they're called, right?"

Dec rolled his eyes and Ian suppressed a grin. "Yeah," Ian murmured. "That's what they're called."

"I'm gonna go talk to her," Dec said.

"I talked to her once," Marcus said. He held out the small medallion he'd found in the barn a few years back. He now wore it around his neck on a leather string. "I showed her this. And I told her about the treasure."

"She's not interested in your silly old treasure," Ian said.

"Yes, she was. When I showed her, she wanted me to tell her all about it. And I told her if she ever wanted to borrow my good luck charm, she could just ask." He paused. "I think she likes me."

"Not as much as she's gonna like me," Dec said. "I'm going down there."

"Dec, don't," Ian pleaded. "She'll figure out we've been watching her."

"Who made you the boss of me?" Dec asked.

"Ian is the boss," Marcus said. "Da made him the boss before we left and we're supposed to listen to him. And if he says—"

"I listened," Declan interrupted. "But that doesn't mean I have to do everything he says." He grinned. "I'm gonna ask her out. Maybe take her to a movie."

"You are so full of shite," Ian scoffed. "She'll never go out with you."

"We'll see." Dec dropped lightly to the ground and waded through the deep perennial beds until he stood on the grass beside Kitty. He glanced back up at Ian who watched him with barely concealed awe. Ian had always been more careful around girls, but Dec had never thought caution was much use. There was no denying that he appreciated a pretty girl, so why pretend otherwise?

He possessed a natural charm that usually appealed to the girls who he found worth pursuing. Girls had become his special talent, ever since he'd first tongue-kissed Alicia Dooley behind the rectory when he was eleven. Since then, he'd kissed a lot of girls. But he'd never approached a girl as worldly and sophisticated as Kitty Donahue. She was seriously out of his league.

But he was thirteen now and he considered himself experienced, enough that a girl like Kitty might just find him interesting. Declan cleared his throat and she glanced over her shoulder.

"What do you want?" she asked, her voice tinged with boredom. "You're in my sun."

"What are ya readin'?" he asked.

"*Jane Eyre*," she replied.

"Interesting?" He approached the blanket and sat down in front of her, then took the book from her fingers. "Would I like it?"

"It's really not a book for blokes," she said. "It's romantic."

Declan nodded as he examined the back of the book. "Blokes can be romantic."

She laughed. "When were you ever romantic, Declan Quinn?"

"I wasn't. Just said I could be if I wanted to be. So what would it take?"

"For what?"

"For you to go out with me?" Dec asked. He'd learned it was always best to use the element of surprise. And to display complete confidence, even if the odds of her agreeing to a date were astronomically low. If he caught her off guard she was more likely to think he'd done this before—and say yes.

"A lot more than you have," she said.

"Like what?"

"A car for one," she said. "I'm not going to be ridin' around town on the back of your bleedin' bicycle."

"I have a car. And a chauffeur," Declan said with a grin. "It's a Rolls, you know. All the big rock stars have 'em."

She considered his point for a long moment, as if the thought of riding around in his grandmother's Rolls Royce appealed to her. "What about nicker?" she asked. "I'd expect you to take me somewhere nice and that will cost."

"I've got money," Dec said. "My nana gives me a big allowance and I never spend it all. I suppose I'd even have enough to buy you some flowers, or some candy."

"Well, aren't you a cheeky little hoor." She tipped her head to the side. "Do me up, will ya?"

Carefully, Dec reached down and picked up the straps that fastened the back of her bikini together. He slid the hook through the loop, then glanced over to the trees, wondering what Ian was thinking. The skin on Kitty's back was smooth and warm from the sun. When he finished, she sat up and readjusted her top until everything was properly covered, though not quickly enough to avoid giving Dec a nice view of her perfect breasts.

She wrapped her arms around her legs. "So, where are you going to take me?"

He dragged his gaze away from her chest and sent her a charming grin. "Wherever you want to go."

"To supper," she said. "At a nice place, with table linens and fancy silver. And then to the flicks. And after that, a ride around the city."

"And when would you be likin' me to take you on this date?" Dec asked.

"Friday evening. You can pick me up at six. Do you know where I live?"

He shook his head. "But I'm sure I can find out." Dec rose to his feet, then rubbed his palms on the back of his jeans.

She gave him a smile that made his stomach do a little cartwheel. "It's a date then. Friday at six. Now, hump off. And tell your brothers I can hear them up on that wall."

"I'll tell 'em," Dec said. "And I'll see you on Friday."

Kitty stretched back out on the blanket and unfastened her top again, then grabbed her book and started to read. Dec decided to walk back to the house through the garden, leaving Ian and Marcus to wonder exactly what had transpired. If he was lucky, they'd heard it all and would be suitably impressed.

There wasn't a girl in the world he couldn't charm. And it was obvious that Kitty was no exception. She was one of the prettiest girls in her form at school and she was going out with him. He jogged toward the house, but before he reached the door, Ian and Marcus came crashing through the garden gate, both gasping for breath.

"You crazy git," Ian said. "You asked her out, didn't ya?"

Dec nodded. "I told you I would. Did ya hear? She said yes."

Ian braced his hands on his knees and gulped in a few deep breaths. "What the hell does she see in a kid like you?"

"She doesn't see a kid," Dec said. "She sees a man."

"Oh, yeah, right. You're a man, you are. Well, tell me, Mr. Man, what are you going to do when she wants to snog in the backseat of Nana's car? 'Cause that's why she wants to drive all over Dublin with you. And what about when she sticks her hand down yer pants and wants to—"

"What's snog mean?" Marcus asked.

"Never mind," Ian said. "Kitty Donahue is used to goin' with older boys. You better be ready to handle yourself or it'll be a big embarrassment."

Declan frowned. He hadn't really thought about all the things that might go wrong. "I know what I'm doing," he muttered. "And don't go givin' me advice, Ian. You haven't ever been on a date, so what do you know?"

"About as much as you do, little brother." He paused, kicking at the dirt with his toe. "So do you love her?"

Dec shrugged. "Nah. I'm only gonna fall in love once when I'm old. And I'm gonna love her until the end of forever, just the same way our da loves our ma. Until then, I'm gonna mess around with as many girls as I can."

Dec followed Ian and Marcus into the house, glancing back once into the overgrown garden. Kitty Donahue had seen something in him, something she found interesting. Now, he'd just have to make sure he lived up to her expectations.

Even if he did mess up, the experience would have to count for something. By the time he was eighteen, Dec fully intended to have women figured out from top to bottom, inside and out. There'd be no guy alive who would have more women, except maybe James Bond.

1

SHE CAUGHT HIS gaze from across the room. Declan Quinn glanced over his shoulder at the beautiful blonde in the slinky blue dress. She gave him a seductive smile, an unspoken invitation to approach, and Dec let his gaze drift lazily from her face to her tanned and lithe body.

Her dress, cut low in the front, left her arms and shoulders tantalizingly bare. Though the length fell slightly below her knee, a deep slit offered a view of a well-toned thigh. From the moment she'd entered the party, they'd been caught in this silent dance, two strangers…interested…attracted.

Declan was never one to shy away from any interest from the opposite sex. But tonight, it could be no more than a casual attraction. Besides, it was obvious what she was looking for. From the huge diamond on her finger and the old man on her arm, she'd settle for a quick roll in the hay with a man half her husband's age.

Dec had a strict policy of never mixing business with pleasure, no matter how stunningly attractive and warmly willing that pleasure might be. He was here in Newport to do a job, to provide security for Edward and Eva Winslow's annual garden party. Screwing one of their guests in the hall closet just wasn't considered professional behavior.

Dec's cell phone buzzed in the pocket of his linen trousers and he snatched it out, turning away from the doe-eyed beauty. "Declan Quinn," he murmured as he stepped off the terrace and into the house.

"Hi, Dec, it's Sally Hughes over at Bonnett Harbor P.D. Your brother asked that I call you."

"Is everything all right?" Dec asked, an uneasy feeling rushing over him. His older brother, Ian, was the police chief in their hometown of Bonnett Harbor, a small village across the waters of Narragansett Bay from Newport. "Are my folks all right?"

"Sure, sure," she said. "I'm calling about Eden Ross. She's been spotted over at the Sandpiper Motel. As far as we can tell, she called in a report of a car theft in progress in order to slip away from some tabloid press. We sent Delaney and Wilson over there and they're holding the reporters. I figured if you'd like to talk to them, I'll have them brought to the station."

"Where's Eden Ross?" Dec asked.

"She and the guy she was with slipped away sometime after our officers arrived."

"Let me talk to Ian," Dec said.

"I'm afraid he's busy. He's got a couple of agents from the FBI here on some art forgery case."

Dec cursed softly. Just yesterday he'd had Ian in his office in Providence along with an art expert. Somehow, his brother had gotten mixed up with Hector Arantes, a known art forger, and Hector's beautiful daughter, Marisol. The case had obviously taken a turn now that the

FBI was involved and Ian would have no time to help Declan track down Eden Ross.

"Call your guys and tell them I'll meet them at the Sandpiper," he said. "I'll be there in ten minutes."

He snapped the phone shut and turned for the door, then felt a hand on his arm. "You're not leaving, are you?"

The blonde slowly circled him, placing herself between him and the door. She leaned into him, her hips pressing against his suggestively. Dec forced a smile. "Business calls," he said.

"There are more important things than business," she said, her fingers sliding down his arm to touch his hand.

Dec chuckled. If he wanted her, he could have her, probably right underneath her husband's nose. They could find an empty bedroom, lock the door behind them, and go at it for ten or fifteen minutes. Or they could make plans to meet later that evening, maybe at a discreet motel across the bay. Hell, there had been a time in his life when he would have welcomed sex without strings. But not now, and definitely not tonight.

"As much as I would like to indulge," he said, "I'm afraid I can't. First of all, I'm chasing a runaway party girl around New England and if I don't find her, her father is going to cancel the million-dollar retainer he gives me to take care of his security needs. Secondly, I just recently promised my two brothers that I'd be celibate for three months and I don't intend to break that promise. And thirdly, your husband is watching us right now and I certainly don't want to have to knock him to the ground when he decides to defend your honor with his fists. There's an obliging waiter passing out champagne over by the pool. I'm sure he'd be willing to satisfy your needs."

She gasped softly as Declan turned and walked toward the front of the mansion. As difficult as it was to turn down a night in bed with a beautiful woman, he did have to keep his priorities straight. After all, he was the one who had challenged his brothers to the celibacy pact and he'd made it three weeks without a regret.

But then, the first week he'd been occupied with tracking down an embezzler for a client in Boston. The second week, he'd been conducting background checks for a client in New York City. And all of this past week had been spent chasing Eden Ross. Celibacy wasn't too difficult if a guy didn't have time to think about sex.

Declan spent the next few minutes coordinating security for the rest of the evening with the three employees he'd assigned to the party. By the time he reached the front door, his car had been brought around and was waiting. He tipped the valet, then hopped inside the BMW sedan and headed out to the main road.

This was the closest he'd come to finding Eden Ross but once again, she'd slipped through his fingers. Still, he knew she was close by and with a little luck, she'd decide to come home on her own. Chasing silly little socialites really wasn't his forte. And the socialite in question had brought her problems on herself, choosing to appear in a naughty sex tape that just happened to make it on to the Internet.

Trevor Ross was his most important client, so Dec had to make an extraordinary effort. But Ross wouldn't be happy at the latest news, especially since Eden had been seen in Dec's backyard. He flipped on the radio and listened distractedly as he steered the car over the Newport Bridge.

"You're tuned to the Ross Radio Network. It's Saturday night, and this is Simply Sex with Dr. Lillian Devine." Dec frowned, reaching out to pop a CD into the player, but the silken tones of the show's hostess kept him listening a few moments longer.

"We're still on the air with Carl from Los Angeles, California. Carl is wondering how he might spice up his sex life. My advice for you, Carl, is to spend some time focusing on your wife's needs. The best way to increase her desire is to make her feel like she's the only lover you could ever want. Invest in her orgasms. Make sure they're the best they can be. Put aside your own desires until you're certain all of her needs are being met."

Dec found himself captivated by her voice, the way words dripped off her tongue like honey. A shiver skittered down his spine and he groaned. He didn't need to be listening to this, especially considering his determination to control his sexual urges, at least for the next nine weeks.

But he continued to listen as Dr. Devine discussed the physiology of the female orgasm, the benefits of oral sex and battery-operated substitutes, and the top five female sexual fantasies. And when Dec finally reached the Sandpiper Motel, he found himself strangely aroused by all the frank talk. With a soft curse, he flipped the radio off and stepped out of the car.

"A woman with a voice like that should not be allowed to talk about sex," he murmured as he walked over to the police cruiser. "How can she expect anyone to pay attention to what she's saying? She'd be better off at 1-900-talk dirty to me."

For all he knew, Dr. Lillian Devine was probably some frumpy fifty-year-old Ph.D Just the thought was like a bucket of ice water tossed down his pants.

But if she were beautiful and smart, then that would be one of his top five fantasies. She wouldn't even have to be drop-dead gorgeous. Pretty would do, even cute. But smart and sexy was an irresistible combination, one he hadn't enjoyed in a very long time. And if the woman could talk dirty to him, he'd be in heaven. Unfortunately, heaven was off-limits for the next nine weeks.

Delaney and Wilson, the two officers from the Bonnett Harbor police department, stood next to a car parked across the road from the Sandpiper. Dec approached and Delaney gave him a wave of recognition. "Sally said you wanted to talk to these guys."

Dec nodded. "Are you sure it was Eden Ross?"

"They were," Wilson said, nodding to the two men sitting in the backseat of the police cruiser. "And we ran the plate on the Mercedes parked in the lot. It's registered to Trevor Ross. She must have taken the keys with her. They weren't left in the room."

Shaking his head, Dec ran his hand through his hair. "I guess you guys ought to be happy this girl doesn't take up a life of crime. She is one slippery customer." He pulled his cell phone out of his pocket and dialed Trevor Ross's private number. "Mr. Ross, Declan Quinn here. I've got some news on your daughter. It seems she did stop by your Newport house just long enough to steal one of your cars."

Dec heard a curse on the other end of the line. "I want you to bring her and the car back to the house tonight," Ross shouted.

"I'm afraid she slipped by us," Dec said. "But, from what I can see, she's safe."

"Fine. Hell, I'm tired of wasting your time and my money trying to find her," Ross said. "Besides, I have another case I need you to focus on. And it will require your complete attention. Have you ever heard of Dr. Lillian Devine?"

Dec reached into his jacket to pull out his Blackberry, surprised that Ross would bring up the name. "I have," he said. "I just heard her earlier on the radio."

"Her real name is Rachel Merrill and she's one of our most valuable on-air talents," Ross explained. "An important part of our syndication package. I've had my security guys watching over her but she refuses to let them get too close. I don't think she believes the threat is that serious. Now it is."

"How serious?" Dec asked.

"We had a letter delivered to the station tonight that was a blatant death threat. I need you to meet me in my office tomorrow afternoon and I'll have my guys brief you. And then I want you to convince her that a 24-hour-a-day bodyguard is in her best interest."

"How do you expect me to convince her of that?" Dec asked.

"You're a charming guy. You figure it out. I want you on her until this nutcase is caught."

Dec was paid a healthy retainer to be at Ross's disposal, whenever a security concern came up. He listened as Ross gave him more details, putting the afternoon appointment into the PDA along with other relevant information. In truth, Dec had to breathe a silent sigh of relief that he could leave the search for Trevor's wild daughter to others. He hadn't spent four years in naval intelligence and another three building up Quinn Security and Investigations to spend his valuable time chasing silly heiresses around the countryside.

RACHEL MERRILL SLID HER KEY card into the garage door opener then slowly pulled her SUV ahead as the doors to the underground garage opened. She glanced over her shoulder, just to make sure that no one slipped into the garage in the dark. As she looked back, she saw her security detail pull up to the curb and wait. She let out a tightly held breath once the garage door was closed.

"Safe," she murmured to herself. She was on her own now and the detail would be there in the morning to follow her during her daily routine. Rachel sighed. Just having security following her was enough to put her in a constant state of anxiety. She couldn't remember the last time she wasn't uneasy...watchful.

A few months ago, the thought of having a stalker was inconceivable. And at first, she'd brushed off the letters, thinking them to have been sent by an overzealous fan. But then the notes had begun to arrive with more frequency, messages left for her at the station at least two or three times a week. And when she found a letter at her home, she was forced to admit that her safety might just be in danger.

Her boss, Trevor Ross, had insisted she leave her

cozy colonial in the College Hill section of Providence and move into a secure high-rise downtown. So Rachel had agreed, and a month ago, she'd packed her bags and headed to safer ground. Ross had given her a new SUV to drive, the tinted windows providing additional anonymity, and had also assigned her a security detail from his corporate force.

Rachel stopped at the valet booth near the elevators and waited for a few minutes, then decided to park the car herself. When she'd pulled the SUV into her parking spot, she turned off the ignition, then rummaged through her purse for her pepper spray. Though she felt relatively safe with the new location, the 24-hour parking valet, and the lobby security, she took her own precautions.

Rachel still found it odd that she'd attract the attention of a stalker. She'd never considered herself a celebrity. Her radio show, Simply Sex with Dr. Lillian Devine, could at times be controversial, inviting responses from all kinds of weirdos, but a stalker? Then again, perhaps it shouldn't have come as any surprise. Normal, handsome, successful men hadn't been beating down her door. Why not a strange, obsessive stranger instead?

She'd taken her radio name, Dr. Lillian Devine, to protect her reputation as an academic, but it also served another purpose—protecting her privacy. Now, whoever was stalking her probably knew that Rachel Merrill, Ph. D and associate professor of anthropology at Providence University, and Dr. Lillian Devine, radio sex therapist, were one and the same.

She'd always known there was risk that her double life might be revealed. And when Trevor Ross had offered her a syndicated radio show, she'd initially refused. But the money had been too good to pass up. Her life as Lillian Devine could fund more research for Dr. Rachel Merrill, and provide her some of the comforts that a college professor's salary couldn't.

So, every weekend, on Saturday and Sunday night between ten p.m. and one a.m., she hosted a nationally syndicated call-in show and answered any question posed regarding sexual behaviors, fetishes, obsessions, addictions and frustrations. Though she possessed a Ph.D in psychology, Rachel's primary focus had always been more in tune with biology or anthropology—the study of human sexual behaviors. As an expert, she provided her listeners with keen insight into their problems. Last ratings period, her show had become the number four rated syndicated radio show nationwide, a jump of seven spots from the previous quarter.

But now, that popularity came with a price that far outweighed the benefit. She was living like a hunted animal, always looking over her shoulder, frightened of what or who might be waiting in the dark. The police were trying to find the stalker, but they had few leads.

Drawing a deep breath, she opened the door of the SUV and jumped out. As she walked toward the elevator, she turned back to set the alarm on the truck. It was then that she noticed the shadowy figure approaching from her right.

"Miss Merrill?"

Rachel picked up her pace and when she reached the elevator, frantically pushed the button again and again, hoping that the door would open and she could escape.

She wanted to scream, but her adrenaline was pumping so hard, her throat seemed to close. As the stalker got closer, she knew a decision was at hand. Spinning around, she aimed her pepper spray at his head and pushed the nozzle.

Funny enough, her first reaction to his face wasn't fear. Instead, she was immediately struck by how handsome he was. Stalkers weren't supposed to be handsome. Or well-dressed. He held out his hand, as if to stop her, but a wave of panic suddenly overwhelmed her.

He saw the spray coming and he raised his hand just in time to block the stream. But the pepper spray had the desired effect. Just the smell made him cough and sputter and his eyes began to water. Cursing, he bent over at the waist, tugging his jacket up over his mouth and nose.

The bell for the elevator door sounded and Rachel dropped the pepper spray and rushed inside. Just as the door closed, he called her name again. "Leave me alone!" she screamed. "Just leave me alone."

"I work for Trevor Ross," the man shouted, adding a string of curses to the statement. "He sent me."

The door shut and the elevator began to silently rise. Rachel's pulse pounded in her ears and her breath came in quick gasps, but she felt as if she were outside her body. Slowly, her mind began to work again and confusion replaced the panic that had overwhelmed her.

He had been dressed much nicer than the average stalker, although she didn't know exactly what the fashionable stalker wore these days. She imagined a hooded sweatshirt and grubby clothes, not a tailored sport jacket and finely pressed trousers. And his dark hair wasn't shaggy and unkempt but neatly trimmed.

If Trevor Ross had sent the man, what was he doing skulking about in the garage? And how had he gotten inside? She needed some answers. So when she reached her floor, she pushed the button for the garage and the elevator slowly descended. When she got back to the garage, Rachel found him squatting against a pillar, his cheeks wet from tears, his head tipped back. He'd tossed his jacket aside and unbuttoned his shirt.

"Who are you?" she demanded, snatching up her pepper spray and aiming it at him again.

"My name is Declan Quinn," he said, squinting up at her. "I run Quinn Security and Investigations. Trevor Ross has our firm on retainer."

"Why are you here?"

"I've been called in to provide you with personal security. There was a death threat made last night during your radio show. Ross thought I might be able to convince you to accept round-the-clock security. Your security detail was supposed to call you and let you know I'd be waiting here."

Her stomach roiled. "A—a death threat. Why didn't someone tell me?"

"That's why I'm here," he replied.

Rachel wasn't sure what to do. The guy looked trustworthy. And he did seem to know the specifics of her situation. "Let me see your badge," she demanded, her voice shaking.

"I don't carry a badge. I'm not a cop." He reached into his pants pocket and pulled out his cell phone. A tear trickled down his cheek and traced a path along his strong jawline. For a moment, Rachel couldn't take her eyes off of it. "Here. Call Trevor Ross. His number is on my speed dial. He'll explain everything."

She hesitated. If he was working for her boss, then she'd just made a very big mistake. "Why did you come after me?" she asked.

"I was trying to introduce myself."

With a soft oath, Rachel tossed the pepper spray aside and stepped closer. She grabbed him by the arm and pulled him along toward the elevator, the fumes from the pepper spray burning at her own eyes. "You shouldn't have startled me," she scolded. "I'm really jumpy lately. And you came out of the dark. What was I supposed to do?"

"You did the right thing," he admitted.

She stopped short. "I did?"

He nodded. "Your first duty was to protect yourself. And you did."

They got inside the elevator and he leaned back against the wall and closed his eyes. Rachel pulled her jacket up over her mouth and nose and observed him silently, taking her first good look at the man. Her heart skipped a beat as she took in his handsome features, the dark hair casually mussed, the straight nose and strong jaw. Her gaze came to a stop at his mouth and a shiver skittered down her spine.

How could she have ever thought this guy was a stalker? A man as gorgeous as him would have to beat women off with a stick, not chase them around in the dark. She wondered what color his eyes were. It didn't really matter. Regardless of the color, they'd just make him more attractive. "I'm sorry," she murmured.

He glanced over at her, his eyes narrow slits, then shook his head. "You hit me in the chest and the hands. I have to get these clothes off. And it's burning my hands. But if you're going to count on pepper spray as a defense, we'll need to improve your aim."

When the door opened on her floor, Rachel stepped out and the man followed her down the hall, his hand resting on her shoulder. His fingers were warm and gentle and when they slipped down to rest at the small of her back, Rachel felt herself go weak in the knees.

Such a simple, innocent touch shouldn't have affected her so strongly. Perhaps it was all the adrenaline pumping through her body that heightened every sensation. Every nerve in her body tingled and she found herself fantasizing about all the other places he might touch her body.

He'd introduced himself, but for the life of her, she couldn't remember his name. In all the excitement, she'd completely lost her ability to think clearly. Quinn. That was it! But was it his first name or his last?

When they got inside, he gave the apartment a cursory glance. "I've got to get out of these clothes," he murmured. "Where's the bathroom?"

Rachel pointed to the hallway on the other side of the living room. "Down that hall, last door on the left." She watched him retreat. She could count on two fingers the handsome men who'd wandered into her life over the past couple of years. Not that she'd been actively looking for a relationship, but she hadn't been "not" looking for a man. It wasn't supposed to be so difficult. If her talk show had taught her anything it was that there was a match out there for everyone. But then spraying a guy with pepper spray didn't exactly create a great first impression.

She hurried down the hall and stood outside the bathroom door. "Is there anything I can do?"

"Do you have any cooking oil?" he asked through the door.

"I think so." Rachel frowned as she headed to the kitchen. If he'd asked her for cottage cheese she would have felt obliged to provide it. After retrieving a bottle of canola oil, she returned to the bathroom and rapped on the door. When he didn't answer, she pushed the door open.

He stood in front of the sink, bare-chested, his shirt wadded up in the corner. Rachel's breath caught in her throat as she stared at his reflection in the mirror. He was slender, but quite muscular, broad-shouldered with a narrow waist and a flat belly. His trousers hung low on his waist, revealing a trail of hair that ran from his belly to beneath his waistband.

As he bent over the sink, she handed him the oil. He poured a bit onto his hands then rubbed it in. "What are you doing?" she asked.

"Taking away the sting." After he removed most of the oil with a towel, he doused his hands in her facial astringent. "You're supposed to use alcohol, but I think this will do."

"I have a bottle of **vodka**," Rachel offered cheerily.

"I'd prefer Scotch," he said. "On the rocks." His voice was deep and rich, with a slightly cynical edge.

"I—I'll just go get—"

He chuckled softly. "Never mind. I don't drink on the job."

"I could use a drink," she murmured.

"Go ahead. I'll be out in a few minutes."

Rachel turned and walked back down the hall. When she reached the kitchen, she took a bottle of vodka from the freezer and poured a measure into a tumbler, then took a slow sip. This was not how she had expected the evening to end, with a half-naked man in her apartment.

After her show had finished at one a.m., she'd looked forward to a long, hot bath, a good book, perhaps a movie to wind down, and then a decent night's sleep. In truth, that's the best she hoped for every night. But since the letters had started, she hadn't slept much at all. And now, a death threat. What was she supposed to do with that?

Rachel kicked off her shoes and sat down on the sofa, sinking into the down-filled cushions. She tucked her feet beneath her and sipped at the vodka, listening to the sounds of a real live man in her apartment. She closed her eyes and tried to pretend he was here for a different reason—for a romantic reason, that he'd emerge from the bathroom completely naked and aroused and ready to seduce her.

The fantasy was enough to distract her mind from her stalker, but then Rachel groaned and pressed her flushed face into a pillow. After what she'd done, the last thing he'd be interested in was getting cozy with her.

A few minutes later, he walked into the living room. His hair was wet and he'd draped a towel around his neck. His eyes weren't watering anymore and Rachel could see they were a deep shade of blue. She swallowed hard and tried to smile. "Better?" she asked.

He nodded, then plucked at the towel. "I hope you don't mind. My shirt is trashed for now. And I left my bags down in my car. Any chance you have a T-shirt I could borrow?"

Bags. He obviously intended to stay, at least overnight. Who was she to object? Rachel shook her head. "No." In truth, she probably did have something he could wear, but she preferred him half-naked. "If you call the parking valet, he'll get your bags and bring them up."

He sat down across from her and rubbed the towel over his damp head. "How long have you been carrying pepper spray?" he asked.

Rachel shrugged. She didn't want to talk about the stalker. For once, she just wanted to put it out of her mind and relax. She was safe for the time being and she wanted to enjoy it. "What did you say your name was?" she asked, running her finger around the rim of the tumbler.

"Quinn. Declan Quinn."

"And Trevor sent you?"

He nodded. "After the latest threat was called in to the--"

Rachel held up her hand to stop him. "I don't need to hear about it."

"Do you have any idea who might be doing this?" Declan asked.

Her gaze flitted over his body, coming to rest on his hands. They were beautiful hands, well-formed with long fingers and neatly groomed nails. "Are you sure you wouldn't like a drink?" Rachel countered. "I think

I do have some scotch." She got up from the sofa and he quickly rose and grabbed her arm to stop her. His fingers were warm on her skin and she looked down at the spot where he touched her, suddenly unable to breathe. "I—I guess not."

"Sit," he insisted. Rachel did as she was told, only this time, Declan sat down next to her, stretching his arm out across the back of the sofa. "Why don't you want to talk about this?"

"I'd just like to stop thinking about it for a while. I don't know who's behind the letters. I don't know if he's serious or just out to scare me. I've talked to a few thousand people over the past couple of years, so it could be anyone. The police can't seem to find this person and they don't take his letters very seriously."

"They will now," Declan said. "It is serious. He threatened to kill you."

"And that's why you're here? To protect me?"

He reached out to take her hand, and the moment he touched her, she felt a current run through her body. Rachel held her breath, fighting the urge to curl up against his body and fall asleep. "I'm tired." She glanced up at him. "You're going to sleep here tonight?"

"If that's all right with you. I can sleep on the sofa."

"There's a guest room," she offered. "You might find something to wear in there. Mr. Ross keeps this apartment for out-of-town business associates, so maybe someone left something behind. And I'll call downstairs and have them bring your bags up as soon as they can."

She slowly rose, but he held on to her hand, his

fingers weaving through hers. "Are you sure you're all right?" he asked.

Rachel nodded, touched by his concern. "I should be the one asking you that."

"Hey," Declan kidded. "I'm tough. It'll take a lot more than a little pepper spray to stop me."

There was something so perfect about his face, she mused. Handsome, yet boyish, but so focused. Her cheeks warmed with another blush. This was silly. She was treating him like some hero come to rescue her. He was an employee, a bodyguard whose only purpose was to make sure she was safe. As much as she wanted to imagine him as her very own sex slave, it wasn't going to happen.

"Good night," she murmured. With that, Rachel turned and walked to her room. She closed the door behind her and slowly began to undress, dropping her clothes across an overstuffed chair in the corner.

But she couldn't drag her thoughts away from the man she'd left in her living room. Sure, Declan Quinn was handsome and powerfully attractive. He was everything she might want in a lover. The only problem was, Rachel hadn't had a lover in her bed in more than a year and had begun to wonder if she'd ever find another man willing to slip between her sheets.

Intellectually, she knew women could live without sex indefinitely, but the physical ache she felt at times was getting almost overwhelming. She wanted to touch a man's skin, to inhale his scent and feel the weight of his body on top of hers.

Men felt a much greater imperative to enjoy the pleasures of the flesh on at least a weekly or monthly basis.

But a year-long drought was bordering on pathetic. Declan Quinn had probably had sex at least once or twice in the last week, maybe even with two different women.

She could write off her drought as a result of a busy work schedule or a lack of suitable prospects. There had been a few men who seemed like good candidates, but once they found out what she did for a living, they were less than enthusiastic about spending a night in her bed.

Rachel had tried to explain that she wouldn't be judgmental or critical, that even though she was an expert in sex, her persona was more a title the media had given her than an indication of her sexual prowess. In truth, her "book learning" far surpassed her actual practical knowledge. She knew exactly what caused a female orgasm, the physiological process that a woman's body went through, but she'd enjoyed precious few orgasms herself.

She had Declan Quinn at her beck and call for at least the near future. So, if she wanted to explore her options, now would be a good time. Rachel was well aware of what it took to seduce a man—in most cases, not much. Men were much more vulnerable to seduction, able to become aroused with just the thought of sex.

Rachel slipped a thin cotton nightgown over her head, then crawled into bed, pulling the sheets up to her nose. She could walk out into the living room right now, stark naked, and chances were good that Declan wouldn't be able to resist a willing female.

With a low groan, she sat up and punched her pillow. For now, she'd get some badly needed sleep. Her sex life could stay the way it was, at least for the next eight hours. Tomorrow morning, she'd reconsider her options.

"He could be married," she murmured, trying to rationalize her reluctance. "Or seriously involved."

The last thing she needed to deal with now, on top of everything else, was rejection. Especially at the hands of a man as sexy as Declan Quinn.

2

DECLAN SWITCHED OFF the light in the guest room. He carried the pillow and the blanket down the hall, then tossed them both on the sofa in the living room. He could choose to sleep in the comfort and relative privacy of the guest room, but he wasn't a guest. He had a job to do and didn't intend to let any bothersome sexual attraction get in the way.

He flopped down on the sofa, then kicked off his shoes. His hands and chest still stung from the pepper spray, but the effects had nearly worn off and he could see again. His mind flashed with an image of Rachel Merrill and he remembered his reaction when he'd first been able to see her clearly.

He'd known a lot of beautiful women but they'd all been beautiful in a conventional way. Thinking back, they'd all shared the same qualities—long, sexy hair, trainer-toned and tanned bodies, and a wardrobe that seemed designed to reveal as much cleavage as possible.

Rachel Merrill was one of those rare women, a woman who was completely unaware of her beauty. She seemed a bit shy and unsure of herself, which only made her more attractive. The striking auburn hair and porcelain complexion didn't hurt her either. Though she wore her hair in a practical shoulder-length style, the tousled waves made it look as though she'd just spent a wild night in bed.

But it was her mouth that Declan found most attractive, the bee-stung lips that just begged to be kissed. A man could lose his soul thinking about that mouth. Declan tipped his head back and stared at the ceiling. And that body. That perfect, slender body with the delicate limbs and the tiny waist, hidden beneath the conservative clothes.

He groaned softly. It had been three weeks since he'd made the deal with his brothers, a bet that they could all remain celibate for three months, a bet they'd reminded him of just yesterday when they'd met for breakfast. They'd all taken the oath on Marcus's little gold charm and tossed a thousand bucks into the pot to make the competition more interesting.

Until tonight, Declan had been sure he'd win. He'd noticed yesterday that Marcus and Ian were already showing signs of cracking. Though he didn't have any proof that they'd broken the pact, he had his suspicions. The bet doubled if either of them actually had sex before the three months were out, so Declan could win as much as four thousand dollars.

It wasn't the money, though. He could make four thousand in the course of an evening. He'd suggested the deal because he'd reached a point of frustration in his life. Everyone around him was settling down and starting a family—his friends, his cousins, guys he'd never expected to find the perfect mate.

Over the past year, Dec had begun to question whether

he might be missing out on something. He'd never had a relationship that lasted longer than three months, and that had been fine with him, until now. But lately, he'd begun to wonder if there was something wrong with him, if he was supposed to want the white picket fence, the mini-van in the garage and loving wife to come home to every night.

He stood up and unbuckled his belt then let his linen trousers drop to the floor, wriggling his feet out of his socks in the process. Declan slowly walked around the apartment in his boxer briefs, listening to the soft hiss of the air conditioning.

The place was almost sterile, with nothing of Rachel scattered about. He couldn't even appease his curiosity by poking through her belongings. Instead, he wandered over to the windows. The apartment was on the thirty-sixth floor of Providence's exclusive One Ten building, the southeast balcony overlooking the river.

Dec walked into the spacious kitchen and pulled open the refrigerator, hoping to find a cold beer but willing to settle for anything to snack on. He pulled out a bottle of orange juice then found a box of crackers in an adjacent cupboard. But as he was going back to the living room, he heard a soft knock at the door. He set the juice and crackers on the dining room table, then walked over to the door and peered out the peephole. Dec recognized the uniform of the building's security force and he unlocked the door and pulled it open.

The man smiled and nodded. "Mr. Quinn. I've brought your luggage. And this envelope just arrived downstairs. The courier said I was to deliver it directly to you. It's from Mr. Ross. If you have any questions, you're asked to call him in the morning."

Dec took the envelope and the guard set his bags inside the doorway. "Thanks," he murmured. He closed the door and walked over to the sofa, then sat down on the end nearest the lamp. Inside the envelope, he found several file folders. The first was a copy of Rachel's personnel file, complete with press clippings and photos. The second was a copy of an investigation report. Ross had hired a small Providence P.I. firm to check out her stalker and their findings were tucked behind a stack of hand-written notes—notes from Rachel's stalker.

But instead of reading through them, he went back to the first folder and withdrew an 8 by 10 glossy of Rachel. Attached to it was a résumé that was several years old. "Born in New York, New York," he murmured. "April 18, 1977." That made her just a year younger than him. He read down the list of her professional degrees and certifications, her published articles, then scanned for more personal data. But everything in the file related to her work experience.

The sound of conversation drew his attention away from the file and Dec stood and crossed to the door again, listening for people outside in the hallway. But the words were coming from inside the apartment— from Rachel's room. As he walked toward Rachel's bedroom, he assumed she was talking on the phone. But when he stood outside and listened to the senseless babble, he realized she was talking in her sleep.

Dec quietly opened the door to her bedroom and poked his head inside. The bedside lamp was still on, bathing the room in a soft pink light. Rachel lay sprawled on the bed, her limbs tangled in the sheets, her nearly sheer nightgown riding high on her thighs. She seemed agitated, tossing her head from side to side as she mumbled.

He stared at her body, the breath slowly leaving his lungs. The soft mounds of her breasts pressed against the cotton, her nipples visible beneath the thin fabric. His gaze slowly scanned down, to the dark shadow between her legs. Dec knew he shouldn't look, but he couldn't help himself. His curiosity needed to be satisfied, but now that it was, it made it more difficult to put her out of his thoughts.

As he watched her, her distress seemed to grow and he wondered if, even in sleep, she sensed his presence. Dec stepped inside and slowly crossed to the bed. He wasn't sure if he ought to wake her, afraid that she might not recognize him and be frightened. But she was obviously caught in the midst of a nightmare.

He gently took her hand and murmured her name, pressing his lips to the back of her wrist. He gave in to the impulse before he realized it and Dec quickly set her hand down. Suddenly, her eyes flew open and she bolted upright. Rachel looked at him for a long moment, her gaze uncomprehending. Then she relaxed, wrapped her arms around his neck and kissed him full on the mouth.

At first, Dec wasn't sure how to respond. But a few seconds later, he returned the kiss, his tongue meeting hers in a delicious dance. She pulled him down on the bed, his body covering hers, his hands furrowed in her thick hair.

Declan had kissed a lot of women in his life, but never had a kiss surprised him so. It was crazy and passionate and full of unspoken promise. And as suddenly as it had begun, it ended.

Rachel drew back, her eyes closed, a tiny smile curling the corners of her mouth. "I have to go to the library now," she whispered. She snuggled into the pillows and a moment later, she was fast asleep.

Declan rocked back on his heels and then glanced down at his lap. His reaction to the kiss was instant and intense. He'd never enjoyed such an uninhibited, yet purely innocent kiss. Ironically, Rachel probably wouldn't even remember it the next morning. Perhaps that was for the best, Declan mused. Things were uncomfortable enough between them. He didn't need to have her embarrassed over behavior she couldn't control.

Still, Dec couldn't help but wonder what might have happened had the kiss been real, borne out of conscious thought rather than the haze of a dream. What would have happened if she'd been awake and kissed him. He wouldn't have put up any resistance even though refusing her should have been his standard, by-the-book response.

The hell with the book, Dec thought. Somehow, he didn't think the book applied when it came to Rachel Merrill. If something *did* happen between the two of them, then he'd deal with it. But it was silly to anticipate an attraction that probably wasn't even there. Rachel just didn't seem all that interested.

RACHEL PUSHED UP ON HER elbow and punched her pillow, frustrated by her inability to sleep. She'd slept for three or four hours before being awoken by an odd dream. She'd been at her office and Declan Quinn had been there with her. And she'd kissed him.

She groaned. What did she expect? There was a handsome man sound asleep just a few feet away from her bedroom. Of course her mind would wander to thoughts of him. In truth, she'd spent the entire night thinking about him.

"Don't fantasize about the bodyguard," she muttered, flopping back down into the pillows. He'd been sent to do a job, and though it seemed as if he cared about her, that's what he was paid to do. To think his interest was rooted in attraction was simply deluding herself.

But it was such a delicious delusion, she thought, smiling to herself. Declan Quinn was a gorgeous man. His dark hair was nearly black and he wore it just a bit longer on the top, just long enough for a woman to run her fingers through it when she kissed him.

Her thoughts switched to his mouth and Rachel wondered what it might feel like to kiss him. He'd probably kissed a lot of women. A man who looked like that wouldn't have any shortage of female companions. And that voice, so deep and rich, was designed to seduce, to convince a woman that all she really needed to make her life complete was to strip off her clothes and climb into bed with him.

Rachel hadn't had to imagine what his body was like. His little encounter with pepper spray had offered her a chance to see just what was under his clothes. A shiver ran through her and she sat up again. Tossing the bedcovers aside, she stared up at the bedroom ceiling.

She'd lost enough sleep over the past few weeks worrying about her stalker. It was strange to be kept awake by other thoughts. Reaching for one of her journals on the bedside table, she searched for anything to clear her mind. A nice long article on anthropological research should do the trick.

But she read the same paragraph over and over, her mind returning each time to the man sleeping in her apartment. Rachel rolled out of bed and walked over to the mirror above a low dresser. She stared at her reflection in the soft light from the bedside lamp. Smoothing her hands over the thin cotton of her nightgown, she looked at her figure critically.

Unlike many single women her age, Rachel didn't work out. She hated exercise and hated sweating even more. But though her body might be a bit soft, she still considered it attractive enough to interest a man. A tiny waist, nice hips, and breasts that were just the right size. "Not too big, not too small," she murmured.

She tipped her head to one side. She'd never considered herself beautiful, though. The features of her face, taken individually, weren't that remarkable. But combined, some men might consider her pretty. And then there was her hair.

She ran her fingers through the thick auburn waves, cropped to just above her shoulders, then turned away from the mirror and walked back to the bed. Her hair had always been the bane of her existence, from the time she was a little girl. It never looked as though she'd done much to style it and usually she hadn't.

Rachel knew the effect of physical beauty on sexual

attraction. Every person had a checklist of qualities they looked for in their perfect mate, a list condensed and honed over time. She could be the most beautiful woman in the world and if she didn't fit Declan Quinn's profile, then she was out of luck.

She crawled back into bed, then listened as her stomach growled. That's why she couldn't sleep. She was hungry. Rachel grabbed her robe and pulled it on over her nightgown. She walked out of her room, passing the closed door of the guest room. Pausing, Rachel listened for the sounds of his breathing, but she couldn't hear anything.

When she reached the living room, Rachel realized why. Declan was stretched out on the sofa, dressed only in his boxer briefs. Though he'd grabbed a blanket from the guest room, it lay on the floor beside the couch, just one corner tangled around his foot.

Rachel drew a deep breath and let it out slowly. The only source of brightness in the room came from the kitchen, from the light above the stove that she left on. It was just enough to make out the details of his face and body. She watched him breathe in and out, his chest rising and falling in a slow rhythm.

She walked over to the overstuffed chair opposite the sofa and sat down, tucking her legs beneath her. Slowly, she let her gaze wander over his body. Attraction was such a strange and mystical thing, she mused. She'd met lots of nice-looking, successful professionals over the course of her adult life, but not one of them had piqued her interest the way Declan had.

But was it really him, or was it simply the fact that

she hadn't had a man in her life for such a long time? Men had a drive to find sexual partners on a regular basis. It was part of their physiological and psychological make-up. But Rachel had the same needs, though not quite as urgent or overwhelming.

The thought of a man, naked and aroused, lying beside and on top of her, touching her, invading her body with his... The thought created an ache inside of her, a need she felt compelled to satisfy.

Since the sexual revolution of the sixties, it had become much easier for women to seek out their own pleasure, at least in theory. But in practice, it was quite a different matter. Convincing a man to bed her took determination and resourcefulness.

Rachel knew exactly how to do it, at least by the book. But there was no way to predict whether Declan would respond, or whether he'd notice at all. She tipped her head back and closed her eyes. Perhaps this wasn't the right man or the right time. She sighed as an image of him swirled in her mind. Still, she wouldn't know until she tried.

DECLAN SLOWLY OPENED HIS EYES, then became instantly alert to his surroundings. He was in Rachel Merrill's apartment, sleeping on her sofa, the dawn just coloring the sky outside the windows of the high-rise. The papers from Rachel's file were spread out on the floor around him. He pushed up on his elbows and yawned, then froze when he saw the outline of a figure standing next to the chair. Dec's instincts kicked in and he jumped up, ready to defend himself.

It was only after the figure took a step back that he realized he was looking at Rachel. He reached over and turned on the lamp and they stared at each other for a long moment.

"Sorry," she murmured. "I didn't mean to scare you."

"I'm not scared," he said.

Her glaze dropped to his crotch and Dec looked down to find an early morning erection pressing against the fabric of his boxer briefs. He'd been dreaming, a very vivid dream, he recalled. And it had involved Rachel. He reached out and grabbed a pillow, holding it in front of him.

"You don't have to be embarrassed," she said with an earnest look. "It's a perfectly normal physiological reaction. It happens during REM sleep. In fact, you probably have three or four a night without even knowing. You have them when you dream, even if the dream isn't sexual."

"It wasn't," he said.

She shook her head, her hair falling into soft waves around her face. "I wasn't accusing you. Although there's nothing wrong with having sexual dreams. That's normal, too."

"Can we stop talking about this?"

She shrugged and sat down in the chair across from the sofa, tucking her feet up beneath her. "You shouldn't be embarrassed to talk about sex. It's perfectly—"

"I know," Declan said. "Normal."

She nodded. For a long while, she watched him, her unflinching gaze fixed on his face, the intensity of her study a bit unnerving. It was as if she could see inside his head, as if she knew his thoughts before he did. Dec couldn't deny that he'd had more than a few erotic thoughts about Rachel over the course of the night. But what man wouldn't? It was perfectly— He cursed inwardly. "So, I guess you know a lot about sex," he commented.

She tucked her feet beneath her. "Some people would call me an expert. That's how I got into this. I wrote a paper for the journals on sexual addiction and then CNN called me to appear on a few of their talk shows when some celebrities claimed sexual addiction in their divorce proceedings. That's how Trevor Ross found me. He liked the way I sounded and asked if I'd be interested in having my own radio show. The offer was good, so I said yes."

"And that's how you became Dr. Devine?"

"I thought it would be better to take a pseudonym. The university frowns upon pop psychology. I think they believe it might tarnish my reputation as an academic."

"Talking about erections on the radio does seem a bit out there."

"I help a lot of people," she said, a hint of defensiveness in her voice. "You'd be surprised at how many of my listeners are completely undereducated when it comes to sex. I believe we should be open and honest about our sexual desires."

"And what are your desires?" he asked. The question was out of his mouth before he even realized he was thinking it. Dec cursed softly. "Sorry, that's personal."

"No," she said. "We might as well be honest with each other." Rachel paused. "Of course, you probably know how charming you are. And I do find you very attractive."

"I find you attractive," he countered, smiling at her. She was right. It felt good to admit it. "And I was dreaming about you when you woke me up."

Rachel smiled. "See, that wasn't so difficult. Now that we've said it, we understand each other."

"That's it?" Dec said.

She nodded. "Yes."

"I don't think it's that easy. We're going to be stuck together for a few days, maybe even weeks. Don't you think being attracted to each other might cause a problem?"

"Why should it? We're two adults who can control our impulses. Just because we find each other attractive doesn't mean we need to rush off to bed."

"At least not right away," he teased.

She blushed, then giggled softly. "Are you hungry? I could make breakfast for us. I think I have eggs. And English muffins. Or I could make French toast."

"French toast sounds good," he said, noticing how deftly she changed the conversation to suit her.

She walked to the kitchen as Dec retrieved his pants from the floor and tugged them on. He joined her a few moments later, sliding into a spot at the breakfast bar.

"I slept well last night," she said. "I felt safe with you here."

Perhaps she'd been safe from the stalker, Dec mused, but considering his own preoccupation with her, her virtue was definitely at risk. "I heard you talking in your sleep. Were you having a bad dream?"

She glanced up from the carton of eggs she'd opened on the counter. "I don't think so. I don't remember."

"I was reading your file last night," Dec said.

"Did you find it interesting?"

"There wasn't any personal information in there, Miss Merrill."

"Rachel," she insisted. "I think we've gotten past formalities, don't you?"

"Rachel," he repeated. He liked the sound of her name on his lips. He wanted to say it a few more times, pleased with the added level of intimacy it gave them. "Tell me, Rachel. Is there anyone in your private life, an ex-boyfriend, a scorned lover, who might be writing those letters?"

She sat down across from him at the breakfast bar and braced her chin in her palm, toying absentmindedly with a pencil. "I wish it was someone I know, but it isn't. I've tried to come up with a list. I have listeners. I also have clients from a small private counseling practice I maintain and from seminars that I conduct regularly. And then there's my research work at the university which puts me in contact with more students."

"So would you say we're looking at thousands of potential suspects?"

She winced. "Yes. I suppose so." Glancing up at him, she met his gaze. "You're never going to catch this guy, are you?"

"We may just have to go about this another way. Sooner or later, he'll make a mistake and I'll be there to catch him."

"How?"

"First, I'm going to make sure you're never in any danger. From now on, you listen to me when it comes to matters of your own personal security. Understood?"

"It could be a her," Rachel commented as she slid off the stool and continued making breakfast. Dec watched as she focused on beating the eggs in a shallow ceramic bowl. Her hair fell down around her face in pretty waves and every now and then, she glanced up at him as if his attention made her uneasy.

"Why don't we start with boyfriends," Dec suggested. He'd been curious since reading her file the night before. "Do you have a boyfriend now?"

"No," she replied, her answer short and inviting no further probing. "Do you have a girlfriend?"

"No," he replied.

She snatched the bag of bread out of the refrigerator and opened it, then tossed three pieces into the eggs. "You're going to tell me that most stalkers are former boyfriends or lovers. But that's not true in this case."

Dec got up and stood next to her at the stove, watching as she heated oil in the pan. "How do you know?"

She drew a deep breath, then glanced over at him. "Because the men I've been with have been the ones to break off the relationship. I've always been the one to get dumped. That pretty much eliminates the ex-boyfriend theory." Declan watched as her gaze fixed on his mouth. "I did have a dream last night," she murmured. She shook her head, then forced a smile. "So are you the only one who'll be guarding me or will someone else replace you when your shift is over?"

As president of his own security company, Dec rarely

did more than supervise his staff and attend the occasional social event. But after meeting Rachel, perhaps it was time to get back in the trenches and do some real security work. After all, it was good to keep his instincts honed. And if he couldn't find Eden Ross, the least he could do was protect one of Trevor Ross's most valuable business assets. "I'm with you until we find this guy," he said softly, the urge to kiss her growing stronger by the second. "I don't want to trust this to anyone else."

"How will that work?" she murmured. "Will you move in here?"

Dec nodded. "And eat here, and follow you around and keep an eye on anyone else following you around. This person is going to show up sooner or later and I plan to be there."

"And what are we going to do about this?" she asked, her eyes wide.

"What?"

Rachel reached out and placed her palm on his naked chest. Slowly, she let her fingertips skim down to his waist and back up again. The sensation of her touch on his body brought an instant response, causing his shaft to grow hard between them.

"This," she said, pressing her hand to his heart. She glanced down. "And that."

"Like you said, we're both adults. I don't mix business with pleasure and you certainly know the pitfalls of casual sex. So we'll just have to have an understanding that this will go no further."

Rachel let her hand drop to her side, then turned her attention back to breakfast. "I have to go over to the university today," she said. "I assume you plan to come with me?"

"Yep."

Dec busied himself making a pot of coffee as Rachel finished the French toast. As the coffee brewed, he sat back and watched her move about the kitchen with an ease and grace that he found fascinating. Her silky robe clung to her body and offered a tempting view of her legs.

Spending twenty-four hours a day with Rachel could hardly be considered work, but it would test his will-power. And resisting the urge to kiss her would be a chore. He'd just have to remind himself he was here to do a job. And that job did not include seducing Rachel.

She handed him a plate of French toast, then set the syrup down next to his plate. "I'm not much of a cook," she said. "If it's bad, you can have cereal."

"It looks good," Dec said.

Rachel sat down beside him and dug into her food. As she bent forward, her robe gaped open and offered a tantalizing view of her breasts. She was so intent on eating that she didn't notice his interest.

"So," she murmured, between bites. "Tell me something. When you masturbate, do you prefer to use magazines or porno videos?"

Declan gasped, hot coffee going down his windpipe. He coughed, unable to catch a breath. He cleared his throat and tried to stop his eyes from watering. "What?"

"Sorry," she said. "I guess I should have saved that question for dinner. It's just that I've been doing research on the subject and I'm curious to get your perspective."

"Why don't we save the discussion for the evening

meal." He shook his head. Talking about sex on the radio had obviously eliminated any inhibitions Rachel had about bringing it up in casual conversation. Dec couldn't help wondering if she'd participate in an equally relaxed manner. Did her open attitude extend beyond the radio airwaves to the bedroom?

He took another bite of his French toast, then washed it down with a swig of coffee. This wasn't going to be easy resisting her rather unusual charms. Especially since she seemed determined to expose every sexual secret he possessed. Talking about sex had never been a turn-on for him before, but he found himself curiously aroused by it now.

Perhaps he ought to appease his curiosity, just kiss her once and rid himself of this attraction to her. It would be so simple to just pull her into his arms and have at it. Maybe then, he could get his mind back on the job at hand, guarding Rachel's body instead of lusting after it.

At the next available opportunity, he'd consider the tactic. After all, it would be for her own good.

3

RACHEL TUGGED THE cotton dress over her head and smoothed it down along her hips. She stared at herself in the mirror, trying to be completely objective about her appearance. She wasn't drop-dead gorgeous, but she did have a pretty face and a nice body. And, in general, normal men should be at least mildly attracted to her.

Declan Quinn was attracted to her, he'd admitted that. And he was far from normal. He was every woman's fantasy—handsome, charming, strong, and without a huge ego to get in the way. Since the moment she'd touched him in the kitchen, Rachel had decided that she'd find a way to get him into her bed.

For a long time, she'd been waiting for the right man to walk into her life. But as the months had passed, Rachel had begun to worry that she'd ever enjoy the pleasures of a man's body. Perhaps it was better to opt for an occasional one-night stand while she waited.

It wouldn't be difficult to get Declan to surrender. She knew the physiological effects of a woman's touch, how the sensation of her hand on his skin went racing through his synapses, the neurotransmitters releasing endorphins and giving his brain its cue to feel pleasure.

Men had natural instincts they couldn't deny and she

knew exactly which buttons to push to send those instincts into overdrive. But she'd never used that knowledge to deliberately seduce a man. In a way, it seemed unprofessional. Could she truly enjoy a night in bed with a man who'd been so easily led?

"Of course you could," she muttered. Rachel sighed and stared at her reflection in the mirror. "It's time you start to practice what you preach, Dr. Lillian Devine." She raked her fingers through her hair, then touched up her lipstick. She'd spoken at length on the radio about the various techniques that humans used for flirtation and today, she'd put those techniques to good—

Rachel stopped short, then closed her eyes. This man was supposed to be her bodyguard. And for a few short minutes, she'd forgotten why he was really there. Again, the fear prickled at her thoughts and she forced herself to think of other things. Maybe thoughts of seducing Declan were simply her mind's way of coping, of relieving the constant stress of her situation.

Still, this attraction between them wasn't imagined. She'd courted his attention by spraying him in the face with pepper spray, an unconventional approach, but it hadn't scared him away. They'd begun talking when she'd offered her apology. She'd made her intentions clear by touching him that morning and admitting her attraction.

If they proceeded in a normal manner, there would be a gradual escalation until their bodies began to synchronize, moving together to caress…to kiss…and finally, to make love. It was all very scientific and quite predictable.

Rachel grabbed her sweater from the bed as she walked out of her room. She expected to find Declan dressed and waiting for her. When he wasn't, she walked to the guest bathroom, finding the door open a crack. "I'm ready," she said. "Are you?"

He pulled the door open and Rachel found him, dressed only in a towel, his face half-covered with shaving cream. "I'm sorry," he said with an apologetic smile. "I got caught up on the phone. It'll just take me a few minutes."

Rachel nodded, then pulled the door closed. But at the last minute, she let go of the knob and it gaped open. From her vantage point in the hall she could see Declan's reflection in the wide mirrors that lined the wall behind the sink.

She made a silent study of his body, for the first time having the time to fully appreciate it. Muscles shifted and bunched across his back as he leaned over the sink, bracing one hand on the countertop. Rachel's fingers twitched as she imagined the feel of his skin, warm and smooth, with hard muscle beneath.

He tipped his head back as he shaved his jawline. There was something so erotic about his task, though it was nothing more than an everyday occurrence to most men. It was patently masculine, something that Rachel had never fully appreciated. In truth, she could spend hours watching him shave and never really get bored.

Her gaze dropped to his waist, so narrow, then his hips. The towel rode low and when he bent forward, she could see the curve of his backside outlined by the soft terrycloth. Rachel knew she was invading his privacy, but she couldn't help herself. There was something about Declan's body that captured her attention. Every detail seemed to spark her deepest fantasies.

He straightened, then ran his hand through his hair and an instant later, the towel dropped to the floor. Rachel held her breath, growing slightly dizzy as she did. Oh, he was beautiful. He stepped away from the mirror to turn on the shower and she caught a full frontal view. A tiny moan slipped from her throat and he turned.

Frantic, she pressed her fingers to her lips and stepped away from the door. A few seconds later she heard him turn on the shower. Emboldened, Rachel stepped back to the door and took another peek. The shower door was clear, letting in the light from the bathroom. Through the glass she could see his outline as he moved beneath the water.

Her gaze ran up and down the length of his body, her attention immediately drawn to the tantalizing curve of his hip and buttocks. Researchers always focused on the physical beauty of the female form and its effect on the male of the species, but very few had acknowledged that the male body was just as intriguing.

Rachel felt a warm flush wash over her body and she turned and leaned back against the wall. If she truly wanted to seduce him, then she'd have to be careful. Appearing too eager might result in disappointment. Research had shown that it was always better to prolong the chase, to extend the anticipation until neither party could hold back any longer. She just wasn't sure if time would be her enemy or her friend.

If Declan caught the stalker tomorrow, then there'd

be no reason for him to continue living with her. But if the danger lasted for more than a few weeks, then prolonging the chase would be a bit sadistic. Timing would be crucial to success or failure.

Rachel took a deep breath and focused her thoughts. She wouldn't make the common mistakes that women often made—she wouldn't be too aggressive or too passive, she wouldn't promise what she wasn't willing to deliver, and she certainly wouldn't let Declan call the shots.

The sound of the shower suddenly ceased and Rachel hurried back down the hall to the living room. This would be the most complicated social experiment she'd ever conducted. But if she was careful, she'd get exactly what she wanted—Declan Quinn, naked, aroused, and in her bed.

A few minutes later, she heard him exit the bathroom and a few minutes after that, he appeared, fully dressed in a nicely pressed blue oxford shirt and khaki trousers. He'd combed his hair with his fingers and it stood up in damp spikes.

He walked over to the dining room table and seemed to pick up a leather belt. But on closer inspection, Rachel realized it was a shoulder holster, with a handgun in it.

"You carry a gun?" she asked.

He glanced over at her and nodded. "I will when we're out in public. Just in case." He slipped the holster over his arms, then buckled it in place. "All right," he said, grabbing his jacket. "Where are we off to first?"

She wanted to blurt out "bed," to push him back down the hall toward her room, undressing him as she went. But Rachel cast aside that fantasy. "My office on campus," she said. "I have to check in with my research assistant and pick up my messages. And there should be a few packages waiting for me."

Rachel grabbed her purse and her briefcase, then walked out into the hall to the elevator. A few seconds later, Declan joined her. He'd put on a linen sport coat, part of the wardrobe he'd had delivered to the apartment earlier that morning, the outline of the holster was evident through the fabric.

Though she knew it was there to protect her safety, the gun gave her a queasy feeling in her stomach. Declan was taking her case very seriously and he was a professional. If he needed a gun to protect her, then there must truly be danger. Still, she trusted him to keep her safe. As long as he was by her side, then she could go about her business as usual.

"My office on campus is only a ten-minute walk," Rachel said.

"We're taking your SUV," he said.

"But it's such a nice a day and I thought we could stop and get coffee before we—"

"No stops, no walk," he said. "The vehicle is safer."

His expression, so relaxed just a few moments ago, was now tensed. His jaw was tight and his gaze hard. "We follow my rules, all right?"

She stiffened her spine and crossed her arms beneath her breasts. "All right. But don't think you can just order me around. You can simply explain why we have to do things your way and I'll understand."

He turned to her. "There may be times I can't explain,"

he said. "I need you to promise me that whatever the situation, if I ask you to do something, you'll do exactly as I say."

"We're both adults and we should both be able to resolve any conflicts we might have with discussion. But we can't if you get bossy."

"I am not bossy," he said. He turned and stared at her, his blue eyes filled with frustration. Declan opened his mouth, then snapped it shut. His fists were clenched at his sides and she wondered if she'd pushed him too far. He probably hadn't slept well last night and now, she was acting like a bitch. But if she was going to spend the next week or two with this man, she wanted to know what made him tick—and pushing him to the edge was a quick way of finding out.

The bell above the elevator door rang and she moved to step inside, but a heartbeat later, she was in his arms, tumbling backwards until they both stumbled to the back wall of the elevator. He turned her around in his arms, pressing her against the wall, the metal rail biting into the small of her back. His body slid along the length of hers until every nerve was aroused and aflame. Declan's lips hovered over hers, his breath warm. "Kiss me," he murmured.

Rachel gasped, stunned by the sudden turn of events. "Is that an order or a request?"

"An order," he said.

His gaze was fixed on her mouth as if he were contemplating exactly how he would attack. She'd temporarily lost the ability to breathe but Rachel didn't need oxygen. "All right," she murmured.

An instant later, his mouth came down on hers in a deep and very thorough kiss. Rachel's knees turned to jelly and she clutched his lapels in her hands just to remain upright. The kiss hadn't exactly come as a complete surprise considering the attraction that had been slowly simmering between them.

But Rachel hadn't even considered that he'd choose this particular moment to give in to his desires. Or that he'd frame it in the form of an order to be followed. She'd determined to remain in control, yet at the very first opportunity, she'd simply capitulated without even an attempt at mounting a defense. Had he asked her to strip off her clothes and dance naked for him in the elevator, she probably would have jumped at the chance.

His tongue teased at hers and Rachel had no choice but to surrender to his fierce assault, wrapping her arms around his neck and furrowing her hands through his hair. Rachel hadn't kissed a man in a long time, but still, she hadn't remembered it being quite so wonderful.

In the past, she'd always over analyzed everything when it came to male-female relationships, from basic flirtation to kissing techniques to full-scale seduction. But for some reason, she didn't feel the need to dissect what she was enjoying with Declan. Instead, she simply wanted to enjoy it.

As he kissed her, his hands wandered over her body, skimming along her spine, smoothing across her hips. The light cotton fabric of her dress was thin enough that she could feel the heat of his palms and the sensation was incredibly arousing. A tiny moan escaped her throat and he drew back.

At first, she thought he was simply coming up for air, but then he stepped away, his hands dropping to his sides. "There," he murmured. "That's better. Now that we've got that out of the way, I can concentrate on work."

"Out of the way?" she asked in a shaky voice.

"You're a client. I have to keep my focus on the job."

"And what if you lose your focus again?" she asked. "Will you kiss me again?"

He considered her question for a long moment, a frown furrowing his brow. He opened his mouth to reply, then snapped it shut, cursing softly.

"You know," Rachel ventured. "I'm really not your client. Trevor Ross is. He's the one who pays you, right?"

Declan met her gaze, then swept her back into his embrace. "Good enough for me," he murmured, his lips soft against hers.

They rode all the way down to the garage without being disturbed and when the doors opened again, Rachel was flushed with excitement, her heart beating wildly and her mind spinning. She wanted to reach over and push the button for the thirty-fifth floor, just so they could ride up and down again. Maybe, given the extra time, they might indulge in something even more intimate.

The valet quickly fetched Rachel's SUV. But when she made to get behind the wheel, Declan gently took her elbow and led her to the passenger side. "I'll drive," he said.

She didn't bother to argue the point. The after-effects of his kiss had completely numbed her stubborn streak. Gosh, she liked kissing Declan. The way he possessed her mouth, gently invading with his tongue and then retreating, caressing her lower lip with his teeth. Just thinking about it sent shivers coursing through her body.

She'd obviously done everything right, provided all the subtle cues that led him to kiss her. He seemed unable to stop himself, overwhelmed by his need to possess her mouth. As she went back over the past few hours, Rachel really couldn't pinpoint what it was that had caused him to ignore his better judgment, but she really didn't care. He'd kissed her, deeply and thoroughly and that was exactly what she'd been hoping for.

When they pulled out of the garage and onto the street, Declan glanced over at her. "I don't know if your stalker is watching us, but when we're in public, I think it would be best if we acted as if we were—"

"Friends?" she asked.

He shook his head. "No. More than friends. Close. Very close. I don't want him to think I'm guarding you."

"Then you want me to pretend you're my lover?" she asked.

"Yes, I think that would be best."

They started off down Westminster Street, then continued across the river to the university. Rachel's office was located in the southwest corner of the Providence University campus. Though she wasn't a tenured professor, she was well-respected by the rest of the faculty in the anthropology department. Her course on human sexuality, taught with Professor Ellsworth from the biology department, was among the most popular on campus and she and Daniel had authored several important articles together. Later that summer, they were scheduled to present the results of a new research study at a symposium in Switzerland.

"How many people know about your double life?" Declan asked.

"No one at the university. My graduate assistant Simon doesn't even know. Most of the people at the radio station do, but they wouldn't say anything. They're all really supportive, from Jim, the station manager right down to Jerry, the intern."

Rachel paused, considering whether she ought to tell Declan about Jerry, then decided against it. The young man had a small crush on her, but Rachel got that from some of her male students as well. They looked at her as a sexually accomplished older woman, the stuff of post-pubescent fantasies.

"There's been a publisher who's been trying to track me down through the station," she continued, "but I told Trevor I wasn't interested in a book deal. And my clients from my private practice aren't aware. If they suspected, it definitely would have come up during their group sessions."

"So your stalker knows where you live and that you work at the radio station. But he hasn't made any contact here at the university?"

A sliver of fear shot through her. Was that what this was about? Revealing Dr. Devine's real identity to the world? "Recently the letters have been sent to the station and the phone messages have been left there. Before that, I got them in my mailbox at home. Then I moved downtown and stopped mail delivery. He must know my real name."

"I'm sure he does," Declan said. "It wouldn't be hard

to find out. He'd just need a computer and a good search engine. And it's only a matter of time before he comes looking for you here."

Panic suddenly exploded inside of her. "You have to stop him," she said. "Before the whole world knows who I really am. This could ruin me professionally. No one will take me seriously."

Declan reached out and grabbed her hand, then pressed a kiss to her wrist. Strangely, the simple show of affection calmed her. He reached out and smoothed a hand over her face, brushing the hair from her temple and tucking it behind her ear. "Don't worry, we'll get him before that happens."

"You're sure?"

"I am."

Rachel sat back in the leather seat and took a deep breath. She'd have to trust that Declan knew what was best. If he asked her to jump off the balcony of her apartment, then she'd do it. If he asked her to eat worms, then she'd comply. And if he dragged her into her bedroom and demanded that she make love to him, then Rachel would have no choice but to do exactly what he wanted.

For now, it was best to follow all his orders without question.

DEC SAT ON THE LEATHER SOFA in Rachel's office and pretended to read the latest issue of the *Journal of Comparative Anthropology*. But in the half-hour that he'd been with Rachel, he hadn't read a word. Instead, his attention was intently focused on Dr. Daniel Ellsworth.

The good professor and Rachel sat at a work table

stacked with books and covered with manuscript pages, the two of them hunched over their latest journal article. Dec's gaze came to rest on Ellsworth's arm, casually draped across the back of Rachel's chair.

From the moment he'd met the man, there'd been an obvious tension between them. Rachel had introduced Dec as her friend and Daniel Ellsworth as her colleague. But it was clear that Ellsworth considered himself much more that that. He took every opportunity to brush against Rachel's body, to touch her hand or pat her back. And to Dec's frustration, she barely noticed.

A soft knock sounded on the door and Rachel's graduate assistant, Simon Lister, poked his head inside. Dec hadn't been too fond of him either, immediately pegging him as a snotty little sycophant.

"Dr. Merrill," Simon said in a nasally voice, "there's a phone call for you. Dean Wilson on line two."

Rachel glanced up. "I'll take it on your phone," she said to Simon. Smiling at Dec, she excused herself and followed her assistant out the door. Dec decided to take the opportunity to get to know Professor Ellsworth a bit better. But to his surprise, Ellsworth began the interrogation.

"So, how long have you and Rachel been seeing each other?" he asked, turning in his chair and stretching his legs out in front of him.

Dec wasn't about to give this guy any information he didn't have to. "Not long," he said.

"What do you do?"

"Rachel and I?" Dec knew what he was asking, but he wanted to see the guy's response.

Ellsworth gave him a haughty smile. "Professionally. What's your profession."

"I guess you could call me a salesman," Dec lied. He turned back to his magazine, hoping that his indifference might irritate Ellsworth. It did.

"You just don't seem like her type," he said.

"What type is that?"

"Intellectual. I always imagined Rachel would prefer an academic. She's so focused on her work."

"Hmm," Dec replied, continuing to read the magazine. "We really don't discuss her work."

Ellsworth gasped. "Her work is very important. Rachel has a great future and I would hate to see her jeopardize it by confusing her priorities. Until she gets tenure here at the university, she has to work very hard to prove herself. And I intend to help her."

"I'm sure she appreciates that," Dec said. He tossed the magazine on the table, then grabbed his cell phone from his breast pocket, distractedly scrolling through the missed calls. "So what do you think of her? I mean, she's hot, right?"

"Hot?"

"Yeah," Dec said. "Hell, the first time I met her I thought, this woman is a total hottie. She was dressed in this—"

"I'm not interested in Professor Merrill's…hotness. She's a colleague."

"But you're a guy. You must have noticed. I see how you look at her. Hey, I don't blame you. There's no harm in looking."

"I'm a happily married man," Ellsworth said.

The moment the words were out of his mouth, Declan knew they were a bald-faced lie. There was no emotion behind the statement, nothing that would make Dec believe Daniel Ellsworth preferred his wife's company to Rachel's. Suddenly, Dec had a suspect, a man who had something to gain from Rachel's fear. Perhaps he'd hoped that she'd confide in him, ask for his help or his protection.

Dec made a mental note to have his staff do a background check on Ellsworth. Every ounce of his experience told him that there was something not quite right about the guy.

"You know, I'm surprised Rachel didn't mention you," Ellsworth said, twirling a pencil back and forth through his fingers. "It's odd, isn't it?"

"Does Dr. Merrill usually confide in you about her personal life?" Dec asked.

"You answered a question with a question. Is there some reason why you don't want to answer my question?"

"Actually, *your* question seemed rhetorical. And I'm wondering why it would make a difference to you."

"I protect Dr. Merrill's interests here on campus," he said. "I look out for her. I make sure she knows everything that's happening, what people are talking about, who's getting grant money, where certain professors are being published next. I consider myself something of a mentor to her."

Dec snatched up another magazine, this time the *Journal of American Psychology,* then tossed it down. "I guess I'm not going to find *Sports Illustrated* in here. Or *Rolling Stone.*"

"Popular culture is the opiate of the masses," Ellsworth muttered, turning back to his papers.

Dec chuckled. "Did you just make that up?"

"No. Theodor Adorno and Max Horkheimer first posited the idea. They said that pop culture is like a factory producing goods designed to manipulate the masses into passivity. Pop culture makes people happy and content, no matter how dire their circumstances."

"Interesting," Dec said, nodding. "Tell me something. Have you been sitting under any trees lately?"

Ellsworth raised his eyebrow. "No."

"That's odd. Because I'm trying to figure out where you picked up that big old stick that's stuck up your butt."

At that moment, Rachel strolled back into the office and smiled at them both. "Sorry, that took a little longer than I anticipated." She walked back to the work table and picked up a page of the manuscript. "Now, where were we?"

Ellsworth shoved his chair back and stood. "Perhaps we should go through this when you don't have any distractions. Call me and we'll meet for coffee." With that, the man strode out of the office, slamming the door behind him.

Rachel glanced over at Dec, a frown wrinkling her brow. "Did you say something to him?"

Dec shrugged. "No. We were just having a pleasant conversation. Getting to know each other. You're aware that he has a thing for you."

"Don't be ridiculous. He's married. I know his wife. Our relationship is strictly professional."

Dec shook his head. "Don't be so sure. I watched

him—watching you. You and him haven't ever been an item, have you?"

"No," she insisted. "We knew each other in graduate school. We used to belong to the same study group. When he heard about the opening here, he called and put in a good word for me. We're colleagues and nothing more. He's a dear friend. And you're wrong if you think he'd do anything to hurt me."

"It's my job not to be wrong about these things. I'm going to have my staff check him out. I want to get a look into his background."

"No!" Rachel cried. "I won't have you digging up dirt on him just to soothe your suspicions."

"What about this Simon guy? What do you know about him?"

"He's my graduate assistant. He has been for almost two years now. Dr. Ellsworth sent him over and he's handling my work very well."

"So he reports to Ellsworth?"

"No, he reports to me. You're acting like this is some conspiracy," Rachel said.

"I know how competitive this academic atmosphere can be. How success is measured by the influence of the people you know. Are you sure that Ellsworth is looking after your interests? Or does he keep you close because of some other motive?"

Rachel grabbed her purse and spun on him. "Enough. I don't care how long you've been doing your job, this time you're wrong. Now, I have other errands to do on campus and then I'd like to get some dinner. If you'd like to stay here, fine. But if you're coming with me, we're not going to talk about this any longer."

Dec followed her to the door, then grabbed her arm and drew her back inside the office. He shut the door and she leaned back against it as he braced his hands on either side of her head. "Does he know you work at the station? Does he know you're Dr. Lillian Devine?" Rachel opened her mouth, then snapped it shut. She didn't need to answer. He could see the reply written on her face. "Why didn't you tell me?"

Rachel ducked under his arm and crossed the office, then leaned up against the work table. "Because I knew you'd suspect him. We were working late one night and we got to talking and I decided to confide in him. He promised he'd never tell anyone and we haven't spoken of it since."

"To your knowledge, he hasn't told anyone."

She bit her lower lip as she considered what he was saying. "Not to my knowledge," she murmured. She sat down on the sofa and tucked her feet up beneath her. Suddenly, Dec regretted being so harsh. Her expression was filled with doubt and confusion—about a person she considered a close friend. "I also told him about my stalker and he seemed genuinely concerned."

Dec sat down beside her and slipped his arm around her shoulders. Rachel leaned into him, resting her head on his shoulder. He sometimes became so intent on doing his job that he forgot she was as confused and troubled about her situation as he was. "I'm sorry," he murmured, pressing a kiss to her temple.

Rachel rested her hand on his chest. "I—I guess there could be a chance," she said.

Dec drew back. "What do you mean?"

"The dean named me to a very prestigious committee about six months ago. Everyone assumed that Daniel would get the position. He was so happy for me. And he really didn't have time to do the work since he has a big research grant he's dealing with."

"All right," Dec said. "At least you're being honest with me now."

Rachel looked up at him and he saw the tears swimming in her eyes. He did the first thing he could think of to make her feel better—he kissed her. Rachel's lips parted and gently, Dec delved into her mouth, enjoying the taste of her.

As they lost themselves in the kiss, Dec realized that it was getting much more difficult to be objective about Rachel's case. His growing affection for her was muddling his brain and distracting his attentions. But he couldn't seem to help himself. She happened into his life and he wasn't about to walk away without exploring the possibilities.

"Come on," he murmured, his lips brushing hers. "I'll take you to lunch."

But Rachel wasn't ready to leave. She pushed up on her knees, then straddled his lap, looking deeply into his eyes. "I don't want to feel this way," she said.

Dec gazed at her pretty face, smoothing his fingers along her cheek. Leaning forward, he kissed her again. "This way?"

She shook her head. "No. Scared. I can't relax. I'm

not sure who I can trust. I thought this was some stranger, but now, I don't know. Now, I'm going to be suspicious of everyone."

"Let me do that," he whispered.

"I just want to get out of here," Rachel said.

"Where do you want to eat?"

"No, I mean out of town. Away from this. I don't have anything going on for the next few days. Tomorrow is the Fourth of July. Can't I just go away and find some place where I don't have to worry about this? I promise, I won't let anyone know where I am. And I'll call in every hour if you want."

Dec shook his head. "Nope. But if you want to get out of town, I'll take you. We'll go back to the apartment, pack a bag and go."

Her expression brightened. "Where?"

"I have a friend with a place up in Maine. Near Southport. It's quiet, private and right on the water. We can spend a few days there. We'll sneak out in my car and I'll have a couple of my guys watch your place while we're gone. Maybe your stalker will get desperate and make a mistake."

Rachel crawled off his lap, her demeanor suddenly much more relaxed. Right now, that's all that Dec could ask for—a way to make Rachel Merrill happy. That had become the most important objective in his life for the moment and for the next few days, perhaps he could relax a bit as well.

4

THEY MADE THEIR ESCAPE without incident, leaving Rachel's car in the underground garage and heading out of town in Dec's BMW. Just to be sure they weren't followed, Declan took a circuitous route out to the interstate. By the time they were headed north, Rachel felt her fears abate.

They passed most of the four-hour drive chatting about inconsequential things—music, books, movies—each of them learning the basics that most couples might cover on the first few dates. In truth, Rachel was glad for the time to know more about Declan—or Dec as he preferred to be called. It only confirmed what she already knew—that he was exactly the kind of man she'd always wanted to meet.

But though the tensions seemed to ease as they got farther away from Providence, Rachel began to wonder whether it was the best idea to spend two nights completely alone in a cabin with a man she found so sexually arousing.

She'd made a decision to take things slowly with Dec, to proceed in a very deliberate manner and not rush headlong into physical gratification. But that plan would probably go out the window once they were stranded out in the middle of nowhere with nothing to do but think about sex, sex and more sex.

"My parents used to bring me to Maine when I was a kid," Rachel said, staring out the window toward the rocky coastline. "They rented a cottage up near Penobscot. My sisters and I used to love those vacations."

"Are your folks still alive?"

Rachel nodded. "My father is a therapist in Manhattan and my mother teaches at Columbia. She's a professor of sociology. I have an older sister who is an orthopedic surgeon in California and another sister who works as an engineer in the aerospace industry. I'm kind of the black sheep in the family."

"You're a professor," he said.

"But not tenured," she said. "And my parents have never really approved of my field of study. They don't consider it very serious or important. I think they hoped I might find a cure for the common cold or discover a new source of energy."

"Why did you choose sex?" Declan asked.

"Human relationships fascinate me," she said. "Especially the battle between intellect and instinct. I started studying animals, but then gradually, I realized that humans were much more interesting."

"So I suppose you hear some pretty crazy things?" Dec asked.

Rachel shook her head. "Some people just look at sex in a different way. Outside the norm. Which doesn't mean they're abnormal, just different."

"You can't tell me a guy obsessed with women's feet is normal."

Rachel shrugged. "You like breasts, he likes feet. What's the difference?"

"Breasts are...breasts," Dec said. "They're sexy and fun to touch."

Rachel slipped her foot out of her sandal, then twisted in her seat, resting her ankle across his thigh. "Go ahead," she teased.

He took her foot in one hand and gently began to massage it. His thumbs worked at the muscles in the ball of her foot, then rubbed at each of her toes. Rachel moaned softly and tipped her head back. "That's very nice," she whispered as she set her other foot on his lap. "Oh, yeah, that feels good. Do the other."

Dec chuckled. "Is this arousing you?" he asked.

"Yes," she teased, tipping her head back again and moaning softly. "Is it arousing you?"

He paused and Rachel opened her eyes, watching him with a playful look. "Yeah, a little," he admitted.

She let her left foot rest between his legs, gently rubbing against his crotch. "How about now?"

He growled softly. "I think you know exactly what you're doing."

"Feet can be very sexual," she said. "The next time you look at my foot, you're going to remember what I did. It will be imprinted on your brain and because it was pleasurable, you'll want me to do it again. And you'll look at women's feet in a whole different way."

He picked her right foot up and pressed a kiss to her instep. "If this is how our little vacation is going to go, maybe we ought to go home right now."

"I think maybe I need to open up your mind a bit more," Rachel said. "Not every paraphilia is strange or dangerous. Some are fun to explore."

"You learn something new every day." Dec smiled, then turned his attention back to the road. Once they reached Wiscasset, they drove over the bridge and turned south, toward Boothbay. Rachel watched for the road marked on the map that would lead to the cabin.

"Whose place is this?" she asked.

"A client's," Dec said. "I installed the security system for him. He lives over in Europe for most of the year, but he said I could come out and use the place whenever I want."

Rachel hadn't had a vacation for years, beyond attending professional symposiums and conferences in the major capitals of the world. She hadn't seen the point of traveling without anyone to share the experience with. Last summer she'd spent her time in Paris sitting alone at cafés, drinking coffee and reading rather than seeing the sights and enjoying the romantic atmosphere.

"So what is there to do around here?" she asked.

"I'm sure we can fish. Jack says there's a small boat we can use. We can swim, though I'm not sure how warm the water will be. The cabin is built on a saltwater inlet. The shore is slab rock, but there's a pier. And it's pretty secluded. We can hike, too."

"I probably should tell you that I'm not very outdoorsy," she said.

"Indoorsy can be good," he said, glancing over at her. Dec steered the car down a narrow dirt drive and slowly, the woods opened up to reveal a rustic log cabin. It had obviously been built recently, but everything had been done to make it look as if it had been a part of the landscape for years.

Rachel gasped. "Wow, this is nice."

He pulled the car to a stop, then jumped out and circled around to open her door. She expected him to pull her along to the cabin, but the first thing he did was yank her into his arms and kiss her. He pressed her back against the car and took his time, exploring her mouth with his tongue, teasing and tasting until Rachel's heart was pounding in her chest.

When he finally drew away, she was breathless and dizzy. "How long have you been waiting to do that?" she asked.

"It was a long drive," Dec said, dropping a kiss at the base of her neck. He grabbed her bag from the backseat, then took her hand and walked along the path to the front porch.

As they climbed the steps, Rachel felt her nerves begin to flutter. There was no going back now. Whatever was going to happen between them, would probably happen here. Now that they were away from her stalker, he didn't have to focus on protecting her. What else was there to do but let their attraction run its natural course? But was she ready to indulge in an affair with this man? She'd known him less than twenty-four hours and all she could think about was seducing him.

He punched a code into the keypad and the door clicked, then Declan swung it open in front of her. Rachel stepped inside and groaned softly as she scanned the interior. It was perfectly quaint and romantic, rustic yet modern, exactly the kind of place she'd picture for a romantic weekend getaway with a handsome man.

"I think we'll be comfortable here," he said.

She wandered around the cabin, then followed a short hallway down to a luxurious bathroom and two large bedrooms. The first bedroom contained a pair of bunk beds and the second had a king-size bed.

Dec rested his head on her shoulder as she stared at the huge bed. "I'll take one of the bunks," he murmured.

"Thanks," she replied, her voice wavering slightly. If they slept together, it would have to be her choice. Dec was a gentleman, that much was clear. But when Rachel was around him, she didn't feel much like being a lady.

He set her bag down at the foot of the bed, then walked back to the large main room. Rachel followed and joined him in the kitchen. "We should run into town and get groceries," he said. "There's a decent grocery store in Boothbay Harbor."

"I think I'd like to take a shower," Rachel replied. She hadn't realized it until now, but she really hadn't had a full night's sleep for a few weeks. And this morning, she'd been up before dawn. "Would you mind if I stayed here?"

"I think you're safe here alone," he said. "Just don't wander off into the woods and get eaten by a bear."

"Would you save me if I did?"

He chuckled. "That's my job, ma'am."

They put together a grocery list, Rachel requesting good coffee, fresh fruit and chocolate. Dec made sure to add beer and wine to the list as well as ice cream. When he was ready to go, he gave her a quick kiss, then headed for the door.

Rachel followed him outside, the screen door slamming behind her, then waved as he drove back toward the main road. When the car had disappeared through the trees, she sighed softly.

The sun was beginning to set over the water and she watched until it dipped below the horizon, then walked back into the cabin. She turned on the lamps on her way to the bedroom, then stripped off her clothes before slipping into her silk robe. Grabbing a pillow, Rachel curled up on the bed and closed her eyes.

If she allowed herself to indulge, this could be a wonderfully satisfying stay. Taking that next step with Declan seemed like the most natural thing in the world. An image of him swirled in her mind, Declan naked, standing behind the glass door of the shower, his body visible but the details blurred. That body had been haunting her thoughts all day long and she couldn't help but lose herself in detailed fantasies. What would it be like to have the chance to touch him, to explore every muscled limb and masculine angle?

Rachel smiled as she let the fantasy take hold, imagining the feel of his mouth on her skin, the soft sounds he made when he kissed her and the delicious strength of his embrace. She'd never completely surrendered to a man, afraid that by doing so, she'd somehow diminish her own identity. But Rachel wanted, just once her life, to feel that complete capitulation, when she let go of all her inhibitions and allowed instinct to take over.

Sex was a powerful thing between a man and a woman, an intimacy that left both partners completely vulnerable. Rachel wanted to see that vulnerability in Dec, to look into his eyes as he buried himself inside her, to watch his face as he climaxed, and then to curl up in his arms and sleep until they were ready to do it again.

She had two days and two nights to make the fantasy a reality. Rachel knew exactly how to seduce him, how to make him want her unconditionally. Every trick that a woman had ever plied in pursuit of a man had been researched and defined and quantified. An expert like her could draw a road map to a night in bed together.

But using her knowledge to make Dec want her seemed a bit manipulative. He ought to desire her for his own reasons, not for the reasons she put into his head. Rachel groaned and rolled over, burying her face in the pillow. She was playing with fire and every moment she spent with Declan, she came closer and closer to the heat.

But the heat felt good and the danger made things even more exciting. Rachel wanted to burn, to let their desire burst into flames and consume them both. And if it left her a little scorched, that was all right. A night with Declan would be worth it.

DEC BENT FORWARD TO scan the contents of the refrigerator. Though he'd come home with bags of groceries, nothing he bought really appealed to him. He'd been lying awake in his bottom bunk for nearly three hours, thinking about the woman sleeping in the bedroom across the hall and wondering what she'd do if he crawled into bed beside her.

Since the moment they'd met, they'd played at romance, kissing and touching, knowing the moment would come when they'd both finally forget their reservations and do what their libidos wanted them to. But Declan couldn't entirely put aside the job he'd been charged to do. Starting a relationship with the woman he was supposed to protect was not the smartest move in the world. They'd have to go back to Providence in a few days and then, he'd return to his role as protector. In truth, becoming Rachel's lover headed his list of really dumb ideas.

But a woman like Rachel just didn't walk into his life every day. Hell, he was even willing to give up the celibacy pact with his brothers for a chance to be with her, and Dec couldn't recall ever deliberately losing a challenge to Ian and Marcus. He'd concede this one though, gladly.

He swung the refrigerator door shut then grabbed a pint of ice cream from the freezer and a spoon from the drawer. He'd returned from his shopping trip ready to prepare a late dinner and enjoy a bottle of wine with Rachel. But he'd found her sound asleep on the bed, curled up like a kitten, a pillow clutched to her body.

The past few weeks had taken their toll on her and for the first time, she could put her worries aside and completely relax. Even if that was all that happened during their stay, it would be worth the trip. So he'd closed the bedroom door and let her sleep.

As he walked out onto the porch, the cool night air hit his skin and he sighed. Though her comfort was important to him, his primary focus was still on catching her stalker. But for the next few days, he'd left that to some of his very qualified investigators. If they did their jobs well and caught the creep, Rachel would be able to return to her everyday life when they returned to Providence.

Strangely enough, he hoped that she'd need his protection for a bit longer. He certainly never expected to enjoy living with her—but he did. He'd never thought he'd be interested in spending all of his time with just one woman—but he did. And though he'd had a few serious relationships in the past, none of them had worked quite like his relationship with Rachel did.

From the moment they'd met, he'd felt completely at ease with her, as if he had nothing to hide. So often, he'd jumped head-first into a relationship, spending the passion and desire quickly before growing bored with what was left over. But now, he was almost afraid to experience further intimacies with Rachel, afraid that there was actually something between them worth exploring.

But what was it? Why did he find her so undeniably alluring? In the past, he'd always felt as if there were someone better out there, just waiting for him. But he couldn't really imagine anyone more beautiful, more interesting, more intelligent than Rachel. And the way she had of cutting right through all the silly bullshit and ridiculous games, of getting to the heart of their attraction, was refreshing. Rachel didn't try to manipulate his emotions and Declan liked that about her.

"You're awake."

He turned to find her standing behind the screen door, her hair tousled by sleep, her silk robe shifted off one shoulder. "I couldn't sleep," Dec said.

"Me, neither," she said. "I had a bad dream. What time is it?"

"Three, maybe four in the morning. The sun will be up before too long."

She smiled as she pushed the door open. "I guess I did sleep. I'm sorry."

"You were lying there so peacefully when I got back, I didn't want to wake you."

She nodded, then crossed the porch to lean up against the railing beside him. She had no right to look so damn beautiful, so incredibly kissable. But she did and there was no way he could deny the desire racing through him.

He turned his attention to the ice cream, uneasy with the need that bubbled up inside of him every time she was near. He scooped out a spoonful and held it out to her. Rachel took the spoon in her mouth and smiled. "Ummm."

A shiver shot through him as her tongue flicked at the corner of her mouth. Dec took a little more ice cream himself, letting it melt in his mouth before swallowing it. He was right to want her, yet at the same time, he knew he shouldn't act on his feelings. Unless Rachel gave him an open invitation, he wouldn't make the first move.

He fed her another spoonful and she looked up at him, her eyes wide, her lips damp and gleaming in the soft light filtering through the cabin windows. "Do you want to touch me?" she asked.

Dec swallowed hard. If that wasn't a sign, then he didn't know what was. He set the ice cream down on the railing, then cupped her cheek in his cool palm. "Yeah," he murmured. "I do." Rachel opened her mouth, but he put his thumb over her lips. "If you tell me that's normal, I'm going to carry you down to the water and toss you in."

Rachel giggled. "I wasn't going to say that."

"Then what were you going to say?"

"Go ahead."

Dec released a tightly held breath as he stood. Reaching down, he untied her robe with clumsy fingers, then pushed it aside. His lips came down on hers and he covered her mouth in a long, deep kiss, their tongues cold and sweet from the ice cream. She sank against him, running her fingers through his hair and opening herself to his gentle assault.

Skin met skin as Dec's hands slipped around to her backside and pulled her closer. She was wonderfully soft and smooth and curvy, everything a woman ought to be. Dec reveled in the feel of her body pressed against his, her breasts rubbing against his naked chest.

She surrendered to every movement of his mouth, opening so that he could taste her more deeply, returning each gentle thrust of his tongue. Her lips invited him to take more, to indulge in something that was fast becoming addictive. Though Dec knew there had to be an end to the kiss, he wanted it to go on forever.

He didn't wait for an invitation to take more. If Rachel didn't want to proceed, then she'd have to stop him. Waves of desire washed over his body as she shoved his boxers lower on his hips, until he could feel her naked belly against his stiff cock.

Dec circled her waist with his hands and lifted her up on the porch railing, then stepped between her legs. Smoothing his fingertips along her shoulders, he brushed at the silk of her robe until it fell away, revealing the full beauty of her breasts.

Though the light was dim, Dec didn't need to see details. Without any barriers, he took his time, enjoying the chance to learn more about her body by touch. "Tell me this is what you want," he murmured.

Her voice trembled as she answered. "Yes. Don't stop."

His desire began to spiral out of control and he drew in a ragged breath and tried to focus. They had all the time in the world, the next few days to explore these feelings. It wouldn't do to rush. He wrapped her legs around his hips and she moved against him, her feet resting on the back of his thighs. He'd need do nothing more than pull her forward and they'd be there, ready to get lost in each others' bodies.

Rachel seemed caught up in the sensation of his touch, her head tipped back, her eyes closed, her breath coming in soft pants. He kissed her again, running his tongue along her lower lip, leaving it damp.

With any other woman, Dec would have known exactly what to do next. Seduction was seduction. There was a certain order to events and then it was over. But with Rachel, he sensed it wasn't quite time for them to consummate this need. From the start, they hadn't done things in the normal fashion and he didn't want to start now.

"Why do I want you so much?" he asked, his voice raw. Suddenly, he wanted an explanation.

She opened her eyes and smiled. "I fit your profile," she replied.

He gently bit her lower lip. "I don't have a profile."

"Yes, you do," she said, running a finger from his chest to his waist and back again. Her hand accidentally brushed the tip of his penis and his breath caught in his throat. "From the moment you were born you began to absorb everything around you, holding on to the things you found pleasing, discarding those you didn't. Sights, smells, sounds. Your mind cataloged them all until it created a perfect mate. And when you find the physical manifestation of those qualities, then you have no choice but to take up the chase."

"And what about you?"

"If I didn't find the qualities I wanted in you, then I wouldn't have let you touch me."

"So it's all that simple?" he asked.

Rachel shook her head. "Actually, that part is pretty complicated. It's the desire that's simple."

Dec slid his palm up to cup her breast, teasing at her nipple with his thumb. "Funny, this doesn't seem simple."

She sighed and tipped her head back. "No, I suppose it doesn't. But what's happening inside our bodies and inside our minds is."

He dipped his head down and ran his tongue over her nipple. Rachel shuddered and then groaned softly. "So what do we do now?" he asked.

"We could have sex," she suggested. "Or we could…"

"Or we could what? We could wait?"

"It's often best to prolong the anticipation," she said. "Find other things to occupy our bodies and our minds. Then, when it does happen, it will be much more intense and pleasurable."

Dec nuzzled her breast, inhaling the scent of her skin, sweet and flowery. He straightened, then dropped a kiss on her mouth. "I'd be silly not to trust the expert, right?"

"Right," she replied. He kissed her neck, sucking gently. "Or maybe not," she added.

He grabbed her waist and set her back on her feet, then carefully retied her robe. Though it took every ounce of willpower Dec possessed to remove his hands from her body, he knew they'd made the right decision. When he made love to Rachel, it wouldn't be just good, it would be incredible. And for that, he was willing to wait a little longer.

They walked hand in hand to her bedroom. Dec kissed her softly as they stood beside the bed, his fingers tangling in her hair. It would take so little to move beyond this, he mused. They could simply lie down and let their desire take over. As if she'd heard his thoughts, Rachel took his hand and pulled him down with her onto the bed.

He stretched out on top of her, his erection pressed between their bodies. She hadn't touched him, at least not as openly as he'd touched her, and for that he was grateful. If she wrapped her fingers around his cock, he knew he'd be lost.

But he could do this, taking everything more slowly, prolonging the chase. It was like sex was brand new again, untarnished by his experiences in the past. He'd never wanted a woman more than he wanted Rachel, but then, he'd never had a better reason to wait.

As they continued to kiss, she pressed her hips against his, gently rubbing until they rocked in a slow, delicious rhythm. He hadn't enjoyed such basic pleasure since he was a teenager, taking his very first steps into the world of sexual experience.

Reliving that first passion made this seem even more intense—and forbidden. He tried to hold back, unwilling to admit that his control was no better than that of a fourteen-year old boy. But as she seduced his mouth with her lips and tongue, Dec gradually slipped into that place where he could no longer control what he felt.

And then, the world shifted and he could no longer hold back. His climax overwhelmed him and he came, spilling his pleasure onto the soft fabric of his boxer briefs. A groan slipped from his throat as the spasms continued and her body arched beneath his.

When he was spent, Dec pushed up on his hands and stared down at her. A tiny smile curled her lips. "You're a very naughty girl," he said.

Rachel nodded.

Dec let his arms collapse and nuzzled his face in the curve of her neck. Then he bit her gently, just enough so that she'd know what she'd done to him. The damp spot between them began to grow and he rolled off of her. His cock was still stiff but the ache to relieve himself was diminished. "The things you do to me," he murmured.

"I figured we could take care of it together or you could take care of it on your own. Either way, you weren't going to get back to sleep until it was taken care of."

"Thank you for thinking of me." He stood and walked to the door of her bedroom, then turned and looked at Rachel, now curled up on the bed hugging her pillow. "This better not be some sadistic game you're playing just to screw with the bodyguard."

"It's not," she said. "Trust me. It will be worth it." Rachel smiled. "Besides, you always have a choice.

You could choose to strip out of those boxers, walk across the room and have your way with me right now. And I wouldn't stop you."

"You wouldn't?"

She shook her head and Dec groaned. This experiment in denial was intriguing, but it was also frustrating as hell. He'd done it all and then some with the women he'd bedded. But he'd never done this. Dec hadn't even thought he was capable. And who knows where it might lead? If Rachel was right and the result between them was the best he'd ever had, then he was willing to wait.

"I'll see you in the morning," Rachel said, her gaze dropping to the damp spot on the front of his boxers.

Dec chuckled softly as he walked out into the hall. This was a hell of a thing to happen between them. It wasn't exactly normal, but it was damn interesting.

He turned and walked to the bathroom. As he cleaned up the remains of his orgasm, Dec caught a glimpse of his reflection in the mirror. He stopped and stared. This was different, he could feel it in his gut. And though he didn't know where it was leading, Dec sensed that it was going somewhere important. Could he be falling in love with Rachel?

He cursed softly. Hell, twenty-four hours ago, she was dousing him with pepper spray. People didn't fall in love that quickly. "Jaysus, Declan, this isn't love," he muttered. "It's just a real bad case of lust."

As he laid down in the narrow bunk, Dec's mind was filled with images of Rachel, her hair brushing his chest, her mouth teasing at his cock, her naked body sitting astride his. It would all happen, and when it did, his feelings would be sorted out. But until then, he'd have to exist in this state of delicious torture—and annoying confusion—for just a little while longer.

RACHEL HAD BEEN UP FOR two hours by the time Dec wandered out of his bedroom. To her relief, he'd decided to put on jeans, rather than wear his boxers all day long. It was difficult enough being around him without having him always walking around half-dressed and completely aroused. Still, he'd neglected to button them up, or put underwear on beneath them, leaving her a tantalizing view of his belly and the dark shadow of hair beneath.

It was odd how they'd managed to be intimate, yet had done it in little fits and starts. She'd seen him naked, but only through the door of the bathroom. He'd seen her naked, but only in the faint light on the porch. She'd touched him intimately, but only with her foot. He'd come, with her help, but they'd both been dressed.

Rachel felt a warm flush color her cheeks at the thought of his hands on her body. He had a way of finding just the right spots on her skin, where the nerves seemed to tingle with anticipation. And when his lips followed his hands, Rachel forgot how to breathe.

"Morning," she murmured, handing him a mug of coffee.

He set the coffee down and stretched his arms above his head, working the kinks out of his back. Her gaze dropped to his belly and then lower, and she wondered if he'd slept in the nude last night. An image of him, lying in bed, sated from his orgasm, the sheets twisted around her limbs, flashed in her mind. She grabbed her coffee and took a quick swallow.

Dec sighed as he leaned over the counter, bracing his arms on the butcher block top. "Did you sleep well last night?"

She nodded. "How about you?"

"Like the dead," he said, a crooked grin playing on his lips. "What exactly happened between us last night? I mean, I know what happened in my boxers, but what happened before that?"

"Desire," Rachel replied.

"I assume you know how that works?"

She nodded and boosted herself up on the counter to sit beside him. "It's pretty straightforward."

He reached over and ran a finger down the outside of her bare leg, then up the inside of her thigh. "Tell me. Why did I want you so much? Why did I want you more than I've ever wanted any woman in my life? And how was it that I was able to stop?"

"You wanted me because of a combination of factors," Rachel replied. "It started with the ice cream."

"How is that?"

"You fed me and I accepted. In the animal world, that's a cue that I'm willing to accept your advances."

"I didn't know that," Dec said.

"You wouldn't. It's hardwired into your brain. Passed down from cavemen. It's instinct at work. You just did it because it felt right."

"So, if I meet a woman on the street and feed her ice cream, she'd want to sleep with me?"

"Not if there isn't desire there in the first place. For us, the timing was right. You probably haven't had a woman for a while and there was a physical need. And I haven't been with a man for a long time, so I reciprocated. Then, there are things standing between us—your job, my job, our pasts, and the fact that we don't really know each other well. Because of that, the need is more acute because it's improper. There's some mystery, which adds to the attraction and makes the chase more interesting. We do share some things in common and we're comfortable with each other, so that adds to it. Finally, we each met the other's profile for a potential lover. When all that adds up, you get desire."

"So, if it's all so cut-and-dried, then how come people make such a mess of it?"

Rachel smiled. "Because desire is blind. We don't always pay attention to the signs. We feel and act before we think."

"Isn't that love? Isn't love blind?"

"That, too," Rachel said. A tiny sliver of guilt shot through her. She wasn't being completely honest with him. In truth, everything he was feeling was based in basic human desire. But what he wasn't aware of was that his feelings could also be the beginnings of love.

"Last night, we felt with our bodies, but we also thought about what we were doing. That's why we stopped before we went all the way."

She was playing a dangerous game. But just because she knew the rules, that didn't mean that she had to give up her chance at something wonderful. In the past, she'd always let love take its own course and look where it had gotten her. Now, she'd found a man who was handsome and interesting and trustworthy, a man who made her head spin and her heart pound. Why not do what she could to make him fall in love with her? How could it possibly hurt either one of them?

Some of her colleagues might consider it manipulative, but Rachel was doing nothing more than any other woman experienced in the art of desire. In truth, there were women out there who were much better at snagging a man than she could ever be. So there was no reason for guilt.

Dec shook his head. "I don't know if I can do that again."

"Maybe you won't have to," Rachel replied.

A long silence grew between them as they looked at each other, their gazes locked. Then Dec slowly nodded and Rachel smiled. "So, what are we going to do with ourselves today?" she asked.

He straightened, then slipped his hands around her waist. "We could go into town and get some breakfast and walk around a little. We could spend the day sunning ourselves out on the pier. We could go for a boat ride or go fishing."

"That all sounds good," she said.

"And we could start by taking a shower together," he suggested.

Rachel pushed up on her toes and kissed him. "All right."

"I was kidding," Dec said. "If we take a shower together, we're going to spend the rest of the day in bed."

"Then we can take a shower later," she suggested.

With that, Rachel turned and walked toward the bedroom, leaving Dec with a confused look on his face.

She grinned. At least she wouldn't have to guess what was going through his mind for the rest of the day.

5

DECLAN TURNED HIS face up to the sun, the mid-afternoon heat warming his skin and relaxing his body. He and Rachel had gone into town for breakfast, then spent the morning wandering along the streets and visiting some of the small shops in Boothbay Harbor.

He'd always hated shopping with women, but shopping with Rachel was actually interesting. She kept him entertained with her droll comments and quirky opinions. And she had a keen knack for knowing when he was becoming bored with the shopping experience, leading him out of the store just before he'd had enough. A waterfront restaurant was the perfect spot for lunch before heading back to the cabin for a lazy afternoon.

The sun was high in the sky when they'd returned to the cabin. They'd headed down to the pier and now lay side by side in a pair of plastic chaises.

"You have a really nice body."

Dec squinted against the sun and looked over to find Rachel watching him. She still wore the skirt she'd worn into town, but now, the skirt was pulled up around her hips. She'd discarded the camisole and was left in just her bra.

"What?"

She sat up and crossed her legs in front of her. "You

have a nice body," she repeated. "The thing I really like about it is that it isn't all pumped up. I don't like men who look…artificial."

"So you think I'm skinny?" he asked.

"No, you're just right. You look like a man is supposed to look. Or at least how I imagine a man is supposed to look. That's all that's really important."

"Hmmm." Dec grinned, then closed his eyes and laid back. "I like your body, too." He paused. "A lot."

"What part do you like the best?" she asked.

"You mean, am I boob man or a butt man?" He sent her another glance, this time letting his eyes wander from her face to her feet. "Stand up."

"No!" she cried.

"How am I supposed to give you an informed answer?"

Reluctantly, she did as he asked. Dec sat up and shaded his eyes with his hand, taking in her slender figure. She held her skirt up and he let his gaze linger on her legs. "It's hard to say," he murmured.

"There's nothing about my body that you like?"

"No, I like everything about it," he replied. "I can't pick just one thing. I like your knees and your shoulders. And the small of your back. And your hair. I like everything about your face, but especially your mouth and your eyes. I'm a big fan of your breasts. And I've grown to appreciate your feet. And your legs are just killer."

She flopped down in her chair. "You're entirely too charming for your own good," she muttered.

"And you're too beautiful for yours," he replied.

A tiny smile twitched at the corners of her mouth and Declan was amazed at how important that smile had become to him in such a short time. Though he took his professional responsibilities very seriously, he'd gone above and beyond his duties by watching after Rachel's happiness as well as her safety.

It was a new and unfamiliar feeling to be so invested in the emotions of another person, especially a woman. Women had always seemed so complicated to him, but not Rachel. When she was upset, it showed, and it didn't take much coaxing for her to reveal why. And when she was happy, his day was perfect.

"I could stay here forever," she murmured.

"So could I." Even a statement like that would have been too much in the past, alluding to promises that he'd never keep. But the truth was the truth. He could imagine staying in this place with Rachel, maybe not forever, but for a very long time.

"I don't have to be back in town until Thursday," she said. "We could stay an extra night. If that's all right with you."

He rolled over on his side, reaching out to run a finger along her arm. "I'd like that."

"You don't need to work?"

"I've got my cell phone. If they need to reach me, they can. Besides, I haven't had a vacation for a long time. I deserve a break."

"You should always take time for yourself," she said.

"When was the last time you had a vacation?" Dec asked.

"Years ago," Rachel admitted. "It's no fun going anywhere alone."

"I agree. But you're not alone this time. And neither

am I." Dec sat up and swung his legs off the chair, then dropped a kiss on Rachel's forehead. "I need to call the office. Can I get you anything while I'm up at the cabin?"

"I'd like another kiss, please," she said.

He bent over her and Rachel grabbed him around the neck, pulling him down on top of her. She wriggled around beneath him until their bodies fit perfectly against each other, then nuzzled his neck. "Thank you for bringing me here," she murmured.

He kissed her and for a long time, he didn't want to stop. Kissing had always been a means to an end for him, a necessary part of seduction. But kissing had taken on a whole new meaning with Rachel. It was just...fun. Like eating candy or riding a roller coaster or curling up in front of a fire on a cold night. A myriad of pleasures awaited him when his lips touched hers and every time they kissed, that revelation was brought home all over again.

When Dec finally got to his feet, Rachel had a satisfied smile on her face. "Bring me something to drink, please?"

"I'll be back in a few minutes. Don't go in the water. Always swim with a partner."

She gave him a crisp salute. "Yes, sir, Captain Safety."

Dec hiked up the small rise to the cabin. He found his cell phone on the counter where he'd left it. He punched in the memory dial for the office and spoke first with his secretary and then with his office manager. Once he'd gone through the daily details of business, he asked to be put through to the investigator he'd put on Rachel's case.

"What can you tell me, Rick?"

"We've done a background check on Daniel Ellsworth. Nothing came up. No extramarital affairs, no gambling debts, no complaints from colleagues. He's very well-respected and according to a few sources on campus, his interest in Miss Merrill is completely professional. They also noted that he benefits from the relationship. According to them, until he paired up with Professor Merrill, he wasn't published in any of the prestigious journals."

"No professional jealousies," Dec asked.

"Nothing out of the ordinary," Rick replied.

"What about her research assistant?"

"Simon Lister is sleeping with his thirty-five-year-old, married landlady," Rick said. "But we're still looking at him. He did have a crush on one of his professors during his undergrad years at Cornell and followed her around for a while. I'll be talking to her tomorrow."

"Were you able to come up with anything on those letters?"

"They were all printed on an Epson printer. Most of the printers at the university are Hewlett Packard. But I sent samples to Sam Devlin over at the FBI and he seems to think the letters were written by a woman."

"He can tell that?"

"He claims he can. Women use words differently than men do, make threats differently. He can't be a hundred percent sure, but that was his opinion."

"So maybe it isn't a guy. Rachel claims she hasn't been involved in a relationship for a while."

"That's the truth," Rick said.

"You checked her out?"

"The info in the file was pretty thin, boss. It made sense."

"So what did you find?" Dec asked, suddenly curious.

"She's had three serious relationships, all with academic types, none lasting longer than a year. Her most recent relationship ended a year ago this last April. Strangely enough, all three of the guys are now happily married."

"All right," Dec said. "Call Trevor Ross and update him. And stay on it. Whoever this person is will probably get a little desperate after a few days of not seeing her. We're going to stay up here through Wednesday night."

"Okay, boss. I'll let you know if we get anything."

Dec closed the phone, then set it back on the counter, surprised by the latest development. If Rachel's stalker was a woman, then that changed the entire complexion of the case. In his experience, women usually stalked because of envy or jealousy, men because of sexual obsession. But that didn't make them any less dangerous.

He decided to keep the newest development to himself. Though he could question Rachel about possible suspects, he'd do so later, after Rick had a chance to gather more information.

Dec grabbed a bottle of lemonade from the refrigerator and strolled back down to the water, thinking about the information Rick had given him. He hadn't thought much about Rachel's past relationships with men. In truth, had any of them lasted, then he wouldn't be where he was today.

Yet, he wondered why other men hadn't found what he had in Rachel. There wasn't anything about her that didn't fascinate him. In his eyes, she was pretty close to perfect. And Dec had never considered himself that much different from regular guys. But then, maybe these eggheads she'd dated weren't regular guys.

Sexy was sexy, Dec mused. Egghead or not, it was the same for all men. And Rachel was definitely sexy. He walked down the dock, only to have his theory proved. Rachel had removed her skirt and was now lying in just her underwear, her panties matching the lacy black bra.

Though her lingerie was less revealing than most bikinis, Dec found it much more arousing. His mind wandered, focusing on how little effort it would take to rid her of the tiny scraps of fabric, just a quick tug here and there and she'd be naked.

"Be careful," he said. "You don't want to burn."

Rachel smiled. "I know. I'm just about done. Even a little sun helps. I don't want to have that pasty look of an academic."

Dec thought her skin looked like perfect porcelain, now with just a hint of pink. "I like your skin, too," he murmured. Rachel sat up and Dec opened the bottle of lemonade and handed it to her.

"I'm going to go up and start dinner," she said. "Are you going to stay down here?"

"For a little while," he said. "Call me if you need help. And be careful, those knives in the kitchen are really sharp."

"There's a broken board on the end of the dock. Aren't you going to warn me that it might bounce up, hit me in the head and cause a traumatic brain injury?"

"Sorry," Dec said. "Just doing my job."

"There are a lot of things you do better than your job," she teased.

As she walked away, Dec twisted in his chair and watched her leave, smiling to himself. He wasn't sure where his protective streak had come from and in truth, it was a bit silly. Rachel had passed twenty-nine years of her life without injuring herself seriously with a kitchen knife or getting a third-degree sunburn. Maybe it was time for him to relax a bit.

He was here, alone with a woman he found incredibly alluring. There were much better things to do than worry.

RACHEL POURED THE LAST OF the bottle of wine into Dec's glass. The remains of their dinner—grilled salmon, asparagus and a salad of baby greens—were scattered across the small table on the porch.

She took a sip of her wine, then leaned back into the cushions of the wicker chair. Try as she might, she couldn't remember a single time when she'd been this content. There always seemed to be some problem plaguing her mind, but tonight, all she thought about was how good the wine tasted and how beautiful the sunset had been...and how handsome Dec looked in the waning light.

The day had passed in lazy enjoyment, both of them aware of what the night would bring. There had been penetrating gazes and innocent caresses, a kiss here and there, little clues that characterized the desire bubbling just below the surface. There was no doubt in Rachel's mind they'd give in to that desire. All they were doing now was marking time.

"If you were back home, what would you be doing?" she asked.

"If I wasn't working, I'd probably be at a pub watching the ball game, or hanging out with my brothers. Or maybe taking a run. What would you be doing?"

"Working," she said. "I used to tell myself that it was good I didn't have much of a personal life, but now I'm thinking I was deluding myself. I love it here. I haven't thought about work since we got in the car and left Providence."

"I probably shouldn't even be here," Dec said, running his finger around the rim of his wine glass. "Especially not with a single, beautiful woman. It's too much of a temptation."

"But that's good," she said.

"No. I'm supposed to be celibate until the beginning of September."

"Are you planning to go into the priesthood or do you have some medical problem?" she asked, taken aback by his confession.

"My brothers and I made a bet that we couldn't go three months without sex. Actually, I'm the idiot who offered up the challenge and they agreed."

It was obvious he'd decided to break his pact. The intimacies they'd already shared were well beyond the boundaries of celibacy. Rachel was pleased that she'd been the one to tempt him. "Sometimes it's good to take a break from sex, to gain perspective on relationships," she commented.

"That's exactly what I said," Dec replied.

"Well, you were right," Rachel said.

"Nah, I was full of shit," he countered. "I should have never made the bet." He drew a deep breath. "I just didn't plan on meeting you."

"Well, you haven't lost yet," she said. "We haven't actually had sex. We've just messed around."

"I wasn't supposed to have any sexual contact with women. No touching, no kissing, no anything, for three months." Dec reached across the table and grazed her jaw with his fingertips. "Now three more minutes is much too long." He stood and drew her up to her feet, then wrapped his arm around her waist. "I can't seem to get enough of you," he murmured, kissing the curve of her neck.

Rachel reached for the buttons of his shirt and slowly undid them. When she was finished, she smoothed her hands over his chest. Bit by bit, inch by inch, they began to explore each other's bodies, slowly pushing aside clothing as they stumbled back inside the cabin.

She nuzzled her face against his chest, then traced a path of kisses to his nipple. Darting her tongue out, she teased at it, bringing it to a hard peak before moving across his chest to the other. He groaned softly, furrowing his fingers through her hair to hold her close.

When she finished, he stole another long, deep kiss and Rachel felt her blood warm and her body relax. Suddenly, her mind became consumed with the sensation of his hands on her skin. She couldn't think, but that didn't matter. With every caress there came an automatic response, a shudder or a moan, an effort to move closer to what they both wanted.

Their mouths still locked, they moved to the sofa and Dec gently laid her down, stretching out beside her. Rachel had never been kissed the way Dec kissed her. He took his time, as if focusing all his seductive powers on her mouth. As his tongue delved inside, then withdrew, she was reminded of what they'd soon share, his hips nestled between her legs, his shaft buried deep inside of her.

A dull ache pulsed at her core and the need seemed to multiply with every breath she took. Rachel rolled over and straddled his body, then tugged her camisole over her head. When she reached around to unhook her bra, Dec sat up and pushed her hands aside.

He slipped his fingers under the straps and let them fall off her shoulders. His mouth found a spot at the base of her throat and he kissed her there, lingering over a pulse as if he could sense her excitement. A moment later, she felt his fingers at her back and the bra fell away.

Rachel shivered in anticipation and when he drew her nipple into his mouth, tiny explosions of pleasure shot through her body. She closed her eyes and allowed her mind to drift, arching against him, inviting him to take more.

He seemed to know her body, sensing what made her moan and tingle and sigh. Though she felt a frantic need, he drew the seduction out, each caress meant to exact the maximum amount of pleasure before moving on to something new.

Rachel's hands smoothed over his wide chest, along the sharp angle of his shoulders and down his muscular arms. His shirt was caught beneath him, hindering his reach and after a time, he grew frustrated with the restriction and twisted out of it.

There was so much more to explore, she mused as she reached for the top button on his jeans. But just as she undid it, a phone rang. Rachel groaned and continued her task, but the sound had broken Dec's concentration. He glanced over his shoulder, then cursed softly. "I should get it," he whispered.

Rachel reluctantly crawled off of him, then smiled. "I'll just finish cleaning up." She grabbed her camisole and tugged it over her head, then walked out to the porch and began to gather the dishes from the small table. Inside, she heard Dec speaking softly on the phone. She couldn't make out what he was saying, but a sudden wave of doubt washed over her. What if he was talking to another woman?

A tiny knot grew in her stomach. She knew he had brothers, that he didn't have time to vacation, and that he did work for Trevor Ross. A man as handsome and charming as Dec probably had plenty of female company. And many of them probably had his phone number. When she'd asked him if he had a girlfriend, he'd said no. Rachel frowned. And if he did have a girlfriend, why on earth would he agree to remain celibate for three months?

Maybe he'd had so much sex over the past year that celibacy sounded good. She laughed softly. Celibacy would never sound good to a man. It just wasn't in their nature to give up sex completely, unless they planned to become a priest or a monk.

And did it really make any difference how many

women he had in his past? This was never supposed to be anything more than a short-term affair, a passionate night or two together before they'd both agree to go their separate ways.

But the better she got to know Declan, the more she realized it might be difficult to give him up. If the sex was fabulous, it might even be impossible. Rachel stacked the dishes in front of her then picked them up and carried them into the cabin. She wasn't going to think about the future. They had two more nights together and that would have to be enough for now. As soon as he was off the phone, they'd pick up where they left off.

Dec was standing in the middle of the kitchen when she went back inside, his cell phone clutched in his hand, his brow furrowed into a deep frown. "That was my office," he said.

"I thought it might be one of your girlfriends."

"I don't have any girlfriends," he said, his expression unchanged.

"Good to know," Rachel replied as she set the dishes in the sink. "Is there a problem at the office?"

"The police just arrested someone in your stalking case. An intern from the radio station. Some kid named Jerry. One of my guys interviewed him earlier this evening and he admitted it."

Rachel gasped. "Jerry? No, Jerry couldn't have done that. He's a sweet kid, he's harmless. He cleans up late at night and I see him during my shift. Every now and then, he brings me coffee. He has a little crush on me. He's just not capable of this."

"He has a crush on you? Why didn't you tell me this? Rachel, you can't keep these—" He stopped and forced a smile. "He admitted it," Dec repeated.

Rachel slowly leaned back against the counter, bracing her hands on the edge. "Then it's over?"

He nodded. "I guess so."

"Wow, that was quick." She drew in a deep breath. "I guess that means we don't have to stay here any longer."

He walked over to her and slipped his hands around her waist. "It's too late to drive back tonight and the traffic will probably be murder," Dec said. "Besides, I've had a little too much to drink. We'll stay tonight and go back tomorrow."

Rachel turned back to the sink and began to fill it with warm water. She'd hoped that he'd want to stay longer, but he'd probably stayed away longer than he ought to, especially since this was a job and not a vacation.

Declan ran his palms up her torso and gently cupped her breasts in his hands. "We still have tonight," he murmured.

"Tonight." Suddenly, she wasn't quite sure why she was doing this. Was she really willing to settle for one wild night of sex with this man and then return to her regular life? There were no promises between them, no indication that this was anything more than just lust. "Your job is done now."

Dec gently turned her around, reaching out to shut off the water as he did. He took her face in his palms and gave her a gentle kiss. "This was not part of the job. This just happened and I'm glad it did. I hope you are too because it doesn't have to end here."

She took a ragged breath and fought back the tears that threatened. "It doesn't?"

"Don't be ridiculous." He wove his fingers through hers and pulled her along toward the sofa. "Leave the dishes. I'll do them tomorrow before we go back." Dec sat down and pulled her down beside him. "Now that this is over, maybe we should get some things straight between us," he suggested.

Rachel stared down at her hands, nervously twisting her fingers and knowing that the "let's slow this down" speech was about to be dragged out. She had heard it before. You're getting too attached, things are moving too fast, you expect too much from me. She'd promised herself this time that she wouldn't fall in love, but a tiny part of her already had.

"I know," she said, reaching out for his hand. "This was crazy, the two of us. But it was an affair of opportunity. I never expected anything long term."

"You didn't?"

She shook her head, falling back on an academic explanation for the ache in her heart. "Physical attraction doesn't always translate into a long-lasting commitment. This was just about sex."

Dec sat back, pulling his hand from hers. "So you were just another notch on my bedpost and I was just another chance for you to experiment?"

"We were more attracted because what we were doing was forbidden. Now that it isn't, the attraction won't be so strong."

"Speak for yourself," Dec said. He stared into her eyes, then smiled cynically. "Somehow, I get the feeling that this is a test. That you're just watching me, ready to measure my response." He stood. "The one thing I liked about you, Rachel, was that you didn't play games. I guess I was wrong."

"I'm not playing a game. I'm just being realistic. Can you really tell me that once we go home, we'll continue on like we've been doing for the past two days? No. You'll go back to work, I'll go back to work, we'll have excuses why we can't be together. Occasionally we'll fall into bed, and then it will gradually end."

"Because that's the way it's always happened before?"

"Dec, let's be realistic. We've known each other for two days."

He considered her statement for a long moment, then shrugged. "You're right," he said. "Not a good idea. Better to stop it right now before we make a mistake." He walked to the door, then stood staring out into the night. "I'm going for a walk. I'll be back a little later."

Rachel didn't want him to leave, but in the end, she didn't stop him. The moment the screen door slammed, she let out a tightly held breath and closed her eyes. This was for the best, wasn't it? She'd been so caught up in this whirlwind of desire that she'd never really considered the consequences.

It would be so simple to fall in love with Declan. He'd been her white knight, riding to her rescue, ready to protect her with his own life. Gosh, it was such a predictable response that she was surprised she hadn't seen it coming.

And never mind the fact that she'd manipulated him into wanting her. She'd had her own bad luck with love, but Rachel wasn't sure she'd be able to recover from a bad ending with Dec. It wasn't in a woman's nature to separate sex from love. She'd tried and it didn't work. Maybe, if it had been another man, she would have succeeded. But Declan Quinn was just too much of what she'd always wanted.

DEC WASN'T QUITE SURE how such a promising evening had ended so badly. He cursed his decision to pick up the phone, knowing that the call had been the beginning of the end. A walk in the woods hadn't helped his mood and when he returned, he'd fully intended to straighten everything out with Rachel. After all, she'd always been interested in how he was feeling.

And how was he feeling? Frustrated, confused? A little angry, maybe? He'd been so quick to trust her, so certain that she wasn't like other women he'd known. But Dec realized he might have been wrong. After her behavior tonight, he could call her fickle and capricious and manipulative.

He could also say, in all honestly, that she might just be a little bit confused and he still wanted her more than ever. As he walked back to the cabin, he went over in his mind what needed to be said. But when he got inside, Dec found the lights turned down low and Rachel's bedroom door closed. He walked up to it and raised his hand to knock, but then realized that the closed door was proof enough of her feelings. So he'd stretched out on the sofa in the dark with a cold beer and every intention of getting himself good and drunk.

In the end, he fell asleep midway through the first beer. It wasn't a restful sleep and he hovered near consciousness as images of Rachel flickered in his head. Over and over, he'd wake himself up, more determined to stop thinking about her. And then, he'd lapse into a fitful dream that made him even more frustrated.

He wasn't sure what brought him out of his dreams again. But when Dec opened his eyes, he cursed softly. The clock on the mantel was closing in on three a.m., barely three hours since he'd first laid down. With a deep sigh, he threw his arm over his eyes. The effects of the earlier wine had worn off and Dec considered waking Rachel, getting her packed and leaving for Providence right then and there.

But there was still time to figure out how to salvage something from what had begun between them. Couldn't she see what it would be like for them, Dec wondered. Wasn't she even curious where it might lead? She must have had some pretty nasty experiences with men to blow him off so quickly.

He took a deep breath and let it out slowly, then drew in another and another, consciously trying to relax himself. As he lay perfectly still, Dec slowly realized he wasn't alone. He pulled his arm away and pushed up on his elbow. Rachel stood at the entrance to the hallway, her back against the wall, her eyes closed.

"Are you all right?" he asked.

She jumped, as if surprised to hear his voice, then quickly straightened. "I just came to get a glass of water. I was afraid I'd wake you."

"I wasn't asleep," Dec said.

"I couldn't sleep," she murmured.

She moved toward the end of the sofa, her hands

clutched in front of her and her gaze fixed on the floor. She wore just her camisole and panties and he could see the soft outline of her breasts beneath the fabric. Dec couldn't deny he wanted to take her into his arms and kiss her, to shelter the vulnerable woman he saw before him.

When he held out his hand, he was prepared for her to refuse it. But then she slowly moved closer to take it and he knew what had been said earlier made no difference at all. She still wanted him.

He pulled her down on top of him, stretching her slender body over his until he could feel every inch of her. Her leg slipped between his and he brought his foot up along her hip, bringing them even closer together. Rachel pressed her lips to his naked chest but before she could do more, he raked his fingers through her hair and forced her to meet his gaze.

"Don't mess with me," he warned. "Either you want to be with me or you don't."

"I do," she whispered, an edge of desperation in her voice. She slid up along his body and kissed him softly. "I do want to be with you."

Her belly rubbed against his cock as she shifted on top of him and he felt himself growing hard. His need for her had always been consuming, but after this evening, Dec felt it even more deeply. He ached to bury himself inside her, to lose himself in her heat and damp.

But Rachel had wanted to take things slowly and now he saw the wisdom in that. He'd make her want him as much as he wanted her. He'd drive her so crazy with desire that she'd have no choice but to continue seeing him once they'd returned to Providence. It wouldn't be finished tonight. He'd make sure tonight was just the beginning.

Dec drew her thighs up along his hips, then cupped her backside, running his hands beneath the silky fabric of her panties. The feel of her skin was amazing, perfectly soft and smooth. She sat on top of him and Dec pushed up to sit, his erection pressed against the warm spot between her legs.

He kissed her breasts through the soft cotton of her camisole, holding her close as she arched back. And then, grasping the hem of her shirt, he pulled it over her head, revealing a body that grew more beautiful every time he looked at it.

Rachel wrapped her arms around his neck as he gently brought her nipple to a peak with his tongue. When he'd done the same to both breasts, he trailed kisses back to her mouth. She left him breathless, teetering on the edge, and he was stunned at the power her touch held over him.

Even the most innocent caress—a soft nibble on his ear, her nails raking down his back, her foot sliding down along his calf—sent desire spiraling through his body. And when he didn't think he could take any more, he could. Dec was almost afraid to go further, afraid that the pleasure he ultimately felt would be so profound that it might ruin him for sex with any other woman.

Right now, Rachel was the only woman he wanted and he couldn't imagine it being any other way. Her pleasure was what he wanted to see, her surrender. He grabbed her waist and pushed her back into the pillows on the end of the sofa. Holding her arms above her head, Dec kissed her neck, her long, lovely arms, her fingertips. Then, he began a slow, sensuous trip lower, kissing and nipping and licking until he reached her belly. Hooking his fingers beneath her panties, Dec pulled them down and tossed them aside.

He stared at her for a long moment, her body completely naked, flushed with the excitement of his touch. He'd always appreciated the special qualities of a woman's form, the things that made it so different from his own. To his eyes, Rachel's body was absolute feminine perfection, from her small but full breasts to her narrow waist to the gentle flare of her hips. Everything about her was designed to drive him mad with desire.

His gaze dropped to the neatly trimmed patch of hair below her belly and he reached down and gently parted her lips with his fingers. A sudden cry erupted from her throat and she jerked in response to his touch.

Already, she was hot and damp, as if prepared for him. But Dec had decided that they wouldn't complete the act tonight. Tonight, she would have her pleasure. He dipped his head and ran his tongue along her tight slit. Her eyes flew open and she looked down at him as he settled himself between her legs, his tongue gently working her clitoris.

She was sweet and damp and with every stroke of his tongue, Rachel grew more wild with desire. Her fingers twisted in his hair as she responded, giving him cues to what gave her the most pleasure. Dec brought her close several times, then backed off and let her relax.

He'd never been quite so careful, so attentive to a woman's responses. This was not just a prelude to his pleasure, this was meant to prove something to Rachel. He couldn't be denied. He was the only man who could make her feel this way and she'd be silly to go looking for any other.

He flicked his tongue across her clit again and again and she arched against him. But this time, when he sensed she was close, Dec decided to take her all the way. Gently, he began to suck and her immediate reaction was so strong that he knew he'd found the key to her release.

A few seconds later, she stopped breathing, tensing, her fingers clutching at his hair. And then, in a heartbeat, spasms wracked her body. She cried out, repeating his name over and over as she came, writhing beneath his mouth until she was completely spent. Gasping for breath, she tugged his head away, then laughed in delight.

There was no doubt in Dec's mind that he'd pleased her. She'd want this again and again and each time, he'd make sure it was as good as the first. He slid up on the sofa, until he was stretched out beside her, gently caressing her belly until the last of her orgasm was spent.

She rolled over and faced him, pressing a kiss to his chest. "Now you," she murmured.

"Don't worry about me," Dec replied, gently biting her shoulder. "I'm just fine."

"It's not good to hold it in," she whispered as she tongued his ear.

"Is that the doctor talking or you?"

"Nature requires that men ejaculate at least once every seven to ten days. It's dangerous not to. It's a physiological imperative."

"Gee, I wonder why the nuns never told us about that," Dec joked. "Besides, you forget what you did to me last night. I think I took care of my imperative."

"Let me do this for you," she begged.

Dec stood up and grabbed her hands, pulling her to her feet. He bent and pressed a kiss to her belly, then pulled her along to the bedroom. They tumbled down onto the bed together. At first, all he'd wanted was for Rachel to sleep again, to do away with the temptation of giving in to her demands.

But she was determined to please him and he was left with no choice but to bring her to her peak once again, simply to distract her. Her second orgasm, this one more powerful than the first, did the trick and before long, she was curled up beneath the covers sound asleep, her body relaxed and sated.

Though Dec laid down beside her, he found himself unable to sleep, his mind filled with images of what he could have enjoyed. He slipped out of bed and walked to the bathroom, certain that a shower would relax him. But the very thought of Rachel, her body twisting and tensing against his mouth, was too much to deny.

He stood beneath the shower, the warm water rushing over him and stroked himself until he found relief, fantasies of Rachel swirling in his head, vivid and arousing. This would be what he was left with until he decided the time was right to surrender to her.

Two could play her game and he intended to win— especially since the prize was something he'd been searching a very long time for.

6

WHEN RACHEL OPENED HER eyes the next morning, she wasn't sure where she was. She'd slept so deeply and dreamlessly her mind seemed especially slow to grasp reality. She rolled onto her back and looked at the ceiling until the events of the previous night gradually came to her.

Closing her eyes, she listened to the soft sound of Dec's breathing, just then aware he was beside her in bed. Rachel rolled onto her side and stared at him, her gaze taking in the boyish features of his face. He looked much younger when he slept, his normally serious and watchful expression replaced by a calm beauty that she found stunningly fascinating.

He had the most incredible face, his features in perfect balance—sculpted mouth, straight nose, strong jaw and lashes that would make any girl envious. But his blue eyes were the most devastating feature he possessed, a color so deep and intense that it made Rachel shiver just to think about them.

Her gaze drifted along his body, then stopped at his belly. He was erect, his shaft pushing the fabric of his boxer briefs out into a little tent. Her thoughts wandered back to earlier that morning, to the two incredible orgasms she'd experienced at his hands—and his tongue. She'd expected him to be good—a man as handsome and charming as Declan would have plenty of practice pleasing women. But Dec was beyond good. Rachel knew the limits of her responses and she'd gone soaring past them the moment his tongue began to work.

Everything she'd known about her body, about her own sexual desire, was now useless. Dec had taken her to a level that she'd never experienced before, a place where she lost the ability to rationalize and analyze and was left with nothing but pure instinct. Though she remembered the wild sensation of coming against his tongue, she couldn't quite put together the details of how he'd gotten her there. Only that it had felt absolutely incredible.

It didn't matter, Rachel mused. Next time, she'd pay closer attention. Next time, he'd come with her. She reached out and drew a finger down the length of his penis and Dec didn't move. Emboldened, Rachel carefully tugged the waistband of his boxers down until she revealed the swollen shaft, the velvety skin hot and taut. Without hesitating, Rachel bent over him and took him into her mouth.

At first, he didn't move, but then Declan slowly came awake. He shifted slightly, but Rachel didn't pause, determined to see how immune he was to her seduction. Earlier, he'd been adamant about who would enjoy what. But if she teased him into submission before he was even aware of what was going on, then she'd return some of what he'd given her.

"Oh, God," he murmured. "What the—" He sighed and shifted again. "Oh, yeah. Oh, that feels good."

Rachel glanced up to find him looking down at her, his gaze still hazy with sleep, his hair rumpled. She turned back to what she was doing, anxious to please. He seemed to grow with each stroke of her tongue and Rachel shoved his boxers down to expose the full length of his shaft.

He was big, bigger than any man she'd known, but that didn't frighten her. In truth, it made the anticipation even more intense. It was difficult not to imagine him inside her, filling her, making her moan with pleasure. She ran her tongue along the length of him and heard him suck in a sharp breath, then hold it. Would he stop her? Or was Declan already past the point of no return?

Again, she took him into her mouth, this time deeper, setting up a long, slow rhythm. Though she hadn't had a lot of experience with oral sex, Rachel simply listened to Declan for her cues. He gradually succumbed to the sensations she was causing and could no longer control his reactions, gasping and moaning with each stroke she took, arching on the bed, his hands clutched in the sheets.

"Oh, that feels so good," he murmured.

She increased her tempo slightly and another moan slipped from deep in his chest. His hips rocked in time with her rhythm and she sensed that he was coming close. But Rachel wanted to make him last, to draw his orgasm out as he had done for her.

He reached down and buried his fingers in her hair, urging her to continue, frantically moving with her. And though she tried to slow down, Dec was already there. Uncontrollable spasms rocked his body and she continued to stroke him with her hand as he came.

He jerked a few times, gulping for breath as he gave in to the pleasure that wracked his body. And when it was over, and he was spent, he threw his arm over his head and groaned. "What the hell did you do to me?" he muttered, reaching down to touch the small pool of cum on his belly.

"No more than you did to me," Rachel countered, sliding up to lie beside him.

He raked his hand through her hair, then kissed her. "Is this payback?"

"Just returning a favor." She snuggled against him, throwing her leg over his waist, the dampness of his orgasm sticky on her skin. "So was it as good for you as it was for me?"

He chuckled softly. "Hell, yeah." Dec dropped a kiss on her forehead. "A nice way to start the day. A guy could get to like that a little too much, I think."

"A nice way to end the day, too."

He sighed, distractedly toying with her hair. "We need to go back today," he reminded her. "I need to stop by the Providence P.D. and check out this Jerry guy."

"I thought we could spend the day together."

"We can be together in Providence. If we want to be."

"And do we?" Rachel asked. "Do we want to be together?"

"I don't know," Dec murmured, frowning. "Do we?"

Rachel wasn't sure what to say. If she said yes and he didn't intend to continue seeing her, then she left herself open to a lot of hurt. He was an adult, he could make up his mind on his own. The fact that he wanted her to make up his mind for him was a cop-out. And if he'd been one of her listeners, she would have told him just that.

She always did this, expected more than any man was willing to give. But not this time. She pushed up on her elbow and smiled at him. "I guess we'll have to play it by ear," she said.

Funny how they were so comfortable with the physical attraction between the two of them, but when it went beyond that, they both hesitated. Rachel drew the sheet up around her naked body. "It shouldn't take me too long to pack," she said.

He ran a hand down her arm, then toyed with her fingers. "We don't have to leave immediately. We could lie here for a little while longer. I could return the favor that you returned to me."

"No, I want to get back. I have work and I need to move my things out of that apartment and back into my house. My life can get back to normal now. It's about time." Rachel tossed the sheet aside and crawled out of bed, then wrapped her robe around her body.

She hated this. They'd started out so honestly and simply, both of them wanting the same thing—each other. But now, everything had turned complicated. Suddenly, there were feelings involved—and after just a few days together!

"You should probably take a shower," she murmured, pulling her suitcase from the closet. "And I have to pack."

Dec tugged his boxers back up, then got out of bed and followed her across the room, stepping up behind her. He wrapped his arms around her waist and kissed the curve of her neck. "What's going on in that head of yours?"

"I don't know." She paused. "This was all such a fantasy, coming up here, being together. But now we're going back to our real lives."

"Do you think real life is going to change this thing we have for each other?"

"I don't know," Rachel murmured, her voice wavering. "I guess we'll have to see."

He kissed her again, then walked out of the room. She watched him go, staring at his finely muscled back as he left. Then she shook her head as if to rid herself of the haze of passion that had been obscuring her thoughts the past few days.

Rachel found her purse, then dug through the contents until she found her cell phone. She turned it on, hoping that it was charged, then waited to see if she had a signal. When she did, she punched in the number of her office.

Simon picked up the phone after the second ring. "Professor Merrill's office," he said.

"Simon? It's Rachel."

"Professor Merrill, I've been trying to get a hold of you. I've been calling your cell, but you haven't picked up."

"I—I accidentally turned it off," she lied.

"Professor Ellsworth has been trying to get you as well. The editor for your journal article called and they need the final edits back by the end of this week, not next. Professor Ellsworth said that he won't approve the article without your final input."

"Tell Daniel I'll be in later this afternoon and we'll finish then." Daniel was the only one outside of Trevor Ross's people who knew about her stalker. He'd understand why she hadn't been available. "I'll see you later, Simon."

She hung up the phone, then began to gather her things, trying to turn her thoughts toward the work she had to complete before the next semester began. It was usually so easy to focus on her professional projects, but her mind was easily distracted lately.

Rachel pulled a dress from the closet, then tossed the rest of her things into her bag, not bothering to fold or smooth anything. She let her robe drop to the floor, then tugged the dress over her head. She found a pair of panties in the top drawer and pulled them on, then threw the remainder of her underwear on top of her other clothes.

When she was finished, she zipped up the bag and dragged it out to the hall. She was just passing the bathroom when Declan emerged. His hair was wet and standing in spikes and though he carried a towel, he hadn't bothered to wrap it around his naked body.

She stopped short, then moved to the left at the same time he moved to the right. They went back and forth a few more times, each mirroring the other's attempts to get by. Finally, Dec cursed and grabbed the suitcase, then set it behind him. In the next instant, he grabbed her around the waist and brought his mouth down on hers, kissing her deeply and thoroughly.

He pressed her back against the wall, her arms pinned up over her head, his mouth hot on her skin. At first, Rachel was stunned by the ferocity of his desire, but then she decided she liked it. It was a wonderful feeling to have a man want her so fiercely that he couldn't keep his hands off of her.

The towel dropped to the floor and Dec's hands tangled in her hair. The kiss grew more intense with every second that passed as Dec ravaged her mouth with his tongue. When he finally drew away, he looked down into her eyes. His lips curled into a satisfied smile as he glanced down at his hard penis. "Any questions?"

All Rachel could manage was a breathless "nope" before he turned and walked into his bedroom. The door clicked shut behind him and Rachel fell back against the wall, her knees suddenly weak.

THE RIDE BACK TO PROVIDENCE was so different from the ride up to Maine, Dec mused. The earlier trip had been full of laughter and conversation, good music and, most importantly, anticipation. But all of that had given way to something else on the return trip. Conversation seemed stilted and Rachel seemed horribly ill at ease. In truth, the first two hours on the road were the worst kind of hell Declan had ever experienced with a woman. He'd thought he'd made his feelings clear to Rachel in the hallway, proving to her that no matter where they were, he'd still want her.

But in retrospect, Dec wondered if his little "attack" had done more to scare her than to reassure her of his desire. By the time they'd reached the other side of Boston, Dec had decided to use Rachel's tactics to get her talking. "So," he said. "When I went down on you last night, how did it feel?"

She gasped. "What?"

"Just curious," he said. "I mean, you're not the only one who's allowed to ask questions like that. Just because you're the Princess of Sex doesn't mean I'm not interested in what makes you tick."

"I am not the Princess of Sex," Rachel said indignantly.

"Oh, all right," Dec replied. "The Queen of Sex. Or is it the Empress of Sex?"

"I know what you're doing," she said. "You're baiting me. Well, it won't work."

"You're the one who is always talking about how we should be honest with each other. I want to know how you feel when you come. What do you think about?"

Rachel stared out the car window. "I'm not going to answer that question. I don't think you really want to know anyway."

Dec glanced over his shoulder then quickly switched lanes, before pulling up on the shoulder of the freeway. He stopped the car, then turned to her. "I want to know. I want to know everything about you."

Rachel glanced out the rear window, then looked at him. "What are you doing? Someone is going to come crashing into us. This is a freeway. You can't just pull over for no reason."

"I have a pretty good reason," Dec said. "And I want an answer to my question. Or we'll sit here forever."

"You are such a…oh, you're just so…" She cursed in frustration. "All right, you want to know what I was thinking? I was thinking you were the only man who'd ever taken the time to tend to my needs first. And everything you did, every sensation you made me feel, was something I wasn't going to forget. It was like you just opened a door and I stepped through and now, nothing will ever be the same again."

Dec let out a tightly held breath. "Holy shit," he murmured. Her answer took him by complete surprise. He expected that she'd tell him she felt good, all warm and gooey inside, that when she came she felt the heavens part and the angels sing. But then, he should have known Rachel would be completely and utterly honest with him.

"Holy shit?" she shouted. "That's all you have to say? I just bared my soul to you."

"I—I'm sorry," Dec said. "I didn't really mean that. I'm just...stunned."

"What? You're stunned that you were so good that I'm going to compare every other man to you? Or you're stunned that I told you how I felt?"

"No," he said, desperate to have her understand. "I'm stunned no other man has ever made you feel that way, Rachel. You're a beautiful, smart, sexy woman and if no other man has appreciated you, then you've been hanging around with the wrong kind of men."

She blinked, as if his reply took her by complete surprise. "Oh," she murmured.

"Oh?" he said in a soft, teasing tone. "Is that all you have to say?"

She smiled reluctantly, a pretty blush turning her cheeks pink. "No. That was a very nice thing you said. And I know you're not like other men I've known. I knew that from the start."

"From the minute you got me with the pepper spray?"

"No. After that. When you came out of the bathroom with that towel hanging around your neck. When I saw your eyes."

Dec sat back in his seat. "See there? That wasn't so bad." He put the car back into gear and glanced over his shoulder, then pulled back out onto the highway.

They drove for a while in silence, both of them still contemplating what had just been said. "So, here's how I see things," Dec finally ventured. "We'd be lying to ourselves if we didn't acknowledge the attraction between us. And though things may have begun in an…unconventional manner, there's no reason why we can't just take a few steps back. So, I propose we go out on a date."

"Don't you think we're a little bit past that?" Rachel asked.

"No, I don't. I think it's important we spend some time together, in public, where we can't possibly try to seduce each other, which is what goes on when we're alone."

"And when do you propose we have this date?" Rachel asked.

"How about tonight?"

She shook her head and for a moment, Dec thought she was going to discard the idea outright. "No, that's too soon. If a man asks a woman out, she should get at least four days notice. Any less than that and she'll look too eager, any more than that and he'll look too eager."

"I suspect this is one of those rules you dispense on your radio show?" Dec asked.

"It's a good guideline," she said. "That, and never, ever have sex on the first date." Rachel sent him a smug smile.

"All right. It's Wednesday. That means we can go out on Saturday night."

"I work on Saturday night. My shift starts at ten and ends at one a.m. I have to be at the station by nine-thirty."

"That will give us plenty of time for an early movie and dinner," Dec said. "Perfect. I'll pick you up at your place." He paused. "I don't know where you live. Where do you live?"

Rachel giggled. "I'll show you, since you'll be taking me home." She relaxed back into the soft leather seat of his BMW. "It's going to be nice to get back home. I miss sleeping in my own bed. And having my things around me."

From that moment on, the mood in the car changed. Whatever had been bothering Rachel before had been alleviated and she was her usual candid and witty self. They talked about the date they'd have and he made suggestions for the restaurant while she gave him dating dos and don'ts. In the end, they decided he'd pick the restaurant and she'd pick the movie.

Dec was truly looking forward to spending an evening with Rachel, just talking and enjoying her company, without seduction on his mind. Sure, he'd be thinking about how nice it would be to kiss her or touch her or undress her, but there wouldn't be any possibility of that while they were out in public. And, according to Rachel's rules, not on the first date anyway.

So it would be a simple date, a chance for them to get to know each other a little better, to spend some time talking and laughing, time for him to confirm what he already knew—that Rachel was the most intriguing woman he'd ever met. He'd be satisfied to see where things went from there.

When they turned off the interstate and headed into Providence, Dec was sure things were back on the right track again. He tried to keep himself from pulling the car over to the curb and kissing her, just to make sure. From now on, he'd take more care to make sure Rachel wasn't pressured to feel something she didn't.

Hell, this was new to him as well. He'd always had women waiting in line, willing to do what it took to spend a night in his bed. But in retrospect, Dec realized it hadn't made him really want a woman in a very long time—at least not in the same way he wanted Rachel.

She gave him directions to her house and he steered through the city. Strangely enough, every direction she gave put him on the same route as the one he took from his downtown office to his house in Colonial Hill. To his surprise, they turned down a street just three blocks from his house and Rachel pointed to a pretty two-story colonial surrounded by tall trees.

"That's it," she said. "The white one with the dark blue shutters."

"I can't believe this," Dec muttered, as he pulled in the driveway. "You live here?"

She nodded. "This is the house that sex bought. I used to have an apartment close to the university, but I got this a few years ago when I took the radio job."

"I live three blocks away from here," Dec said. "I run past this house almost every morning. I didn't know you lived here."

"And I didn't know you lived there," she said. "How come I never saw you around the neighborhood?"

"I run early in the morning. I usually spend my weekends with my family in Bonnett Harbor. Maybe we just weren't meant to meet until now."

"Maybe not," she said with a playful grin.

He jumped out of the car and jogged around to Rachel's door, then politely opened it for her. She got out and stretched her arms over her head. "It's good to be home," she said. "I'm going to take a shower in my own bathroom and lay on my own sofa and read my own books. It's going to be strange though."

"How is that?" Dec asked as he fetched her bags from the trunk of the BMW.

"I can relax. I don't always have to be looking over my shoulder. I can go places and do things again. Maybe I'll go to the grocery store. Or for a walk. Or just go out for a drive."

Dec followed her around to the side door of the house, waiting while she found her keys in her purse and unlocked the door. They entered a large kitchen, beautifully decorated with pale cabinets and a granite-covered island, cozy yet airy. This was the first chance he'd had to see how Rachel really lived, to walk around and look at her belongings.

Dec didn't waste any time, setting the bags down next to the door. "Can I look around?" he asked, glancing at her collection of odd refrigerator magnets.

She shrugged. "Sure. I can take you on the tour if you'd like."

Nodding, he took her hand as they walked from the kitchen through a short hallway into the front of the house. They stopped in the foyer and Dec walked over to the front door. The lock system was ancient, an old deadbolt and button lock on the knob, with no reinforcement on the doorframe. He could gain entrance with a shove of his shoulder. "We're going to have to do something about this," he said.

"My door?"

"Your security," Dec replied. "Any halfwit burglar could be in here in less than five seconds." Dec walked over to the window beside the door. "You could use a glass break alarm on this window. If the guy didn't want to expend the effort to bust the door down, he could just break this window and reach in and unlock it. And you should have sash alarms on every window and motion detectors on the first floor."

"But this is a pretty safe neighborhood. And I always lock my doors."

He stepped over to her and took her hand, then kissed her fingertips. "Sweetheart, you're the expert in sex and I have been happy to defer to you on that. But I'm the security expert and this house is a burglary waiting to happen. I'm going to send some of my guys over here tomorrow morning to spec out a system for you."

"All right," she said. "But don't make it too complicated. I can't even program my VCR."

"Don't worry," he murmured, dropping a kiss on her mouth. "It'll come with private lessons taught by the president of the company."

Rachel pushed upon her toes and kissed him and Dec took the opportunity to give her a kiss that would last for however long they were apart. Hell, four days suddenly seemed like an eternity. "Can I call you?" he asked.

Rachel nodded. "Sure. My number is in the book."

"Well, that's going to have to change too," he said,

nipping at her bottom lip. "You should have an un-listed number."

"Stop," Rachel said, giving him a teasing slap on the chest.

He grabbed her face between his hands and kissed her again. "I can't stop," he whispered. "Don't make me." Dec gave her one last kiss, then smoothed his hand through her hair and stepped back. "I should go."

"You'll call me?"

"Yeah. And I might jog by your house a few times a day, just to make sure everything is all right."

"I'll look forward to seeing you run by," Rachel said. "Make sure you're wearing very tight shorts."

Dec chuckled as Rachel unlocked the front door and walked out with him. They stood on the porch for a long moment before she reached out and grabbed his hand. "Thank you," she said, twisting her fingers through his. "For everything. For watching over me. For taking me to Maine. For making me feel safe."

"No problem," he said. "So, I'll see you Saturday?"

Rachel nodded. Maybe there was a chance they could make this work, Dec thought. In the beginning, it had been about the sexual attraction. But now, it looked as if they might share more. He drew in a deep breath. Best not to think too far ahead into the future. He would just take this one day at a time.

And if they ended up in her bed—or his—he'd enjoy the experience, whether there would be a next time or not.

RACHEL PICKED UP THE LAST page of the manuscript and carefully read through the bibliography. She felt as if she was finally accomplishing something today. She'd had all three of her Thursday morning group therapy sessions at her office downtown and then, after a late lunch, she'd come back to campus to catch up on all the work she'd missed.

"I think there's a later edition of that Barrington book," she murmured. "Do you think we should cite that instead?"

"Which book did you use for reference?" Daniel asked.

"The 1963 edition," she said.

"Leave it. If they want to change it, they will."

Rachel handed him the page. "So would you like Simon to type up the edits or are you going to give it to your assistant?"

Daniel chuckled. "Give it to Simon. He's eager to please. And from now on, when you're out of the office for more than a day, be sure to give him a call. He was frantically trying to find you yesterday morning. He called me three times to see if I'd heard from you."

"He's just doing his job," Rachel said.

"I think he's in love with you," Daniel countered.

"Simon? No, I don't think so."

Daniel carefully rearranged the pages of the article. "It's not so difficult to believe," he murmured. "Any man that really knew you would have a hard time not falling in love with you."

Rachel gasped softly, stunned by the look on his face. "Daniel, I—I—"

"You don't have to say anything," he continued. "You don't have to tell me I'm married. You don't have to tell me my wife loves me very much. And that I'd be putting my marriage at risk. I just had to get that out there."

"Were you hoping I'd want something more?" she asked.

He shrugged. "Nope. Because, that would be one of the biggest mistakes I'd ever make. You're a colleague and an old friend and I know better than to put our friendship at risk. But I'm not going to lie to you. There are times, when my marriage is not the best and when I wonder what might have happened if I'd been single when you took this job and you'd been interested."

"I'm sorry," she said. "I just never thought about it. Not because you aren't a great guy, but because you're married."

"And if I wasn't?"

Rachel shrugged. "Well, there is this man I've met and he's—"

Daniel held up his hand. "Say no more. Declan Quinn seems like a charming guy, although I wouldn't have pegged him as your type. But I can see you must care for him."

"How?"

"You look different. Happy. Excited." He set the article on her desk. "How did you meet him?"

"Trevor Ross sent him over last weekend after I got another threatening letter at the station. He was my bodyguard."

"He told me he was a salesman," Daniel said.

"Well, he probably told you that because he suspected you might be my stalker. But they caught the guy sending the letters."

"Who was it?" Daniel asked.

"Jerry Abler. An intern at the radio station. He seemed

like such a nice guy." She frowned. "They're still holding him. I was going to go over and talk to him but Ross's people told me I shouldn't."

"They're right," Daniel said. "It's best to just put this behind you."

"Right," Rachel said. She drew in a deep breath. "So, I guess we're done here."

Daniel nodded, then smiled sheepishly. "Listen, forget what I said before. Just wipe it out of your head. I'm just feeling a little bit battered lately."

"Are you having trouble with Marcy? If you are, I could help you out with that. Maybe find you a marriage counselor."

"I think you're the last person we need helping us out with our marriage," Daniel said. "We'll work it out. But thanks for your concern."

"And thank you," Rachel said. "You know, you're the only person I've told about my work at the station and my little stalker problem. I'm glad I can confide in you. You're a good friend, Daniel."

"I will always be a good friend," he said as he pulled her office door open.

Rachel watched as he left the outer office, a melancholy smile on her face. There might have been a time when Daniel's overture would have been welcomed, before he was married, before she'd met Dec. But now, all she could feel was sad that he was so unhappy in his marriage. Everyone deserved to find that one great passion in their life, the one person who could make life exciting. Maybe Daniel could recapture that with Marcy. Rachel made a mental note to put together some books that might provide help. And get together a list of marital counselors. It was the least she could do for a friend.

Rachel went back inside her office and grabbed the manuscript, along with her purse and her briefcase. She wrote a quick note on top of the manuscript, then dropped it on Simon's desk before she left.

Her car was parked in a surface lot not far from her office and Rachel took her time walking over, enjoying the sense of freedom she now had. She hadn't realized how much having a stalker had affected her life. There had always been an underlying fear in everything she'd done, everywhere she'd gone. And now, that fear had vanished and she felt as if she could live her life again.

Today was Thursday. She had to wait another two days to see Dec, but in that time she planned to shop for a new dress, get her hair highlighted and her nails done, and decide on the perfect movie for them to see. It was strange. She was even enjoying the anticipation of their date, wondering what it would be like to just focus on each other for an evening, without the possibility of seduction surrounding them.

That possibility would probably always be there when they were together, Rachel mused. It was difficult not to think of Dec in those terms. Every time she looked at him, she found herself mentally undressing him, then mentally going through all the things she wanted to do to him once he was undressed. She could play out an entire seduction in her head, from first kiss to final orgasm and Rachel was sure even that fantasy wouldn't live up to the reality.

But there was time for them now and she didn't mind waiting. Waiting would make everything so much more intense once it actually happened. Rachel crossed the lawn to the parking lot, all the while going over the delicious details in her head.

She found her car where she had left it, but as she was unlocking the door, she noticed something odd. A long, deep scratch ran across the lower part of the door. She followed it, only to find that it ran the entire length of the Lexus sedan. Someone had keyed her car!

She knew there had been instances of vandalism on campus, but security kept that to a minimum. As she walked around the car, an uneasy feeling began to set in. Maybe this wasn't a random act of vandalism. Maybe this had been deliberate. She'd never really believed Jerry was her stalker. What if the real one was still out there and the police had made a mistake? They'd ignored her case for so long, perhaps they'd just arrested the first convenient person they'd found.

But Jerry had confessed. Why would he have confessed when he didn't do anything? Rachel groaned softly. She ought to know, since she understood the psychology of interrogation. Jerry had always seemed like such a sweet, shy guy, the kind of guy who got pushed around at the radio station, asked to pull all the worst shifts. When the other interns were out at the clubs on Friday and Saturday nights, Jerry was covering the shifts they were supposed to take.

It was easy for a guy like that to want a little attention. And if he'd been accused of doing something unlawful, perhaps accepting the blame was a way to increase his street cred with his fellow interns. She'd personally seen the way he sought their approval.

"No," she murmured, getting into her car. "This is over. Dec said it was over and he knows what he's talking about. He wouldn't make a mistake."

But as she drove to campus security to report the incident, Rachel's mind began to spin with the possibilities. As she waited at a light, paranoia began to set in and odd little comments niggled at her brain. First, there was Daniel. He'd basically professed his unrequited love for her. Harboring a secret affection could give him every motivation to stalk her. And then there was Simon, who according to Daniel, was also carrying a torch for her. And then there were her clients and her students and her colleagues, any of whom could be concealing a hidden resentment.

Her first instinct was to call Declan and tell him what had happened. But after careful thought, she decided he would probably overreact and lock her up until he was sure she was safe. She'd just gained her freedom again, she wasn't going to lose it due to her own paranoia.

"I'm just tired," she said. "This is all just some post-traumatic panic attack."

Rachel spent the next half hour with campus security detailing what had happened, then headed for home. Security reassured her that they would look into it and informed her that campus cameras may have picked up video proof of the perpetrator.

Satisfied and somewhat calmed, she headed for home. But when she got there, Rachel began to feel uneasy. She'd planned to do some gardening, planting a few flower pots for her porch. But instead, she locked herself inside the house.

As Dec had promised, a crew had showed up that morning to wire her house with alarms, but they wouldn't complete the job for another day or two. She walked back and forth in the hallway, trying to work through her fears, telling herself that they were unfounded.

But the more she attempted to calm herself, the more upset she became. Rachel hurried to the kitchen and picked up the phone, ready to call Declan. She wouldn't tell him what had happened, she'd just call to talk. His voice had a way of calming her. That would be enough.

She snatched her purse off the counter and searched through it for his business card. He'd written his cell phone number on the back, along with his address and his home phone number. She decided to try the cell phone first.

Punching in the number, she said a silent prayer that he'd pick up. Perhaps he'd be ready to head out for a run and she'd suggest he'd stop by for something to drink. Or maybe he was coming home from work and he'd drive by to say hello. Her mind conjured all kinds of excuses for him to come over and allay her fears.

It rang three times before his voice mail picked up. Rachel listened to the message, then hung up before leaving hers. With trembling hands, she set the phone down and stepped away, her need for Declan suddenly overwhelming her.

She'd known him for just a few days, and though they'd spent more time together than many couples who had dated for months, she still shouldn't feel so dependent upon him. Rachel opened the refrigerator and pulled out a bottle of wine, uncorked it and took a drink from the bottle.

"Don't be such a baby," she murmured to herself. "You're just looking for any excuse to see him. If it wasn't the vandalism on your car, you'd find another reason."

She'd thought it was nearly impossible to resist Dec when she was with him. But now Rachel had found it was just as difficult to resist him when she wasn't. Somehow, she suspected that until they were together twenty-four hours a day and enjoying a wild and wonderful sex life, she'd never be satisfied.

7

"DECLAN?"

Dec pressed the button on his phone to activate the intercom. "Yep."

"Your brother, Ian, is here," the receptionist said.

"Send him back, Celine," Dec said, surprised by the impromptu visit. He gathered up the files he had spread over his desk and signed a few letters waiting in the file from his assistant, then walked to his office door and opened it.

His older brother smiled as he strode down the hall. He wasn't wearing his uniform, dressed instead in a faded pair of jeans and a blue work shirt. "Hey there," Ian said.

"Come on in. What are you doing in town?" Dec asked.

Ian flopped down into one of the chrome and leather chairs in front of Dec's desk, heaving a deep sigh as he did. "Just hanging out," he said. "I'm working this weekend, so I figured I'd take the day off."

"So you came to Providence? Just to hang out? On a Friday night? Sounds like you're here looking for women."

"No, I had other stuff to do," he said.

"Care to elaborate?" Dec asked.

"Stuff," Ian insisted. "I had to drop a friend off at the

airport. Hey, thanks again for that help with the forgery case. I haven't talked to you since I saw you and Marcus for breakfast last weekend."

"No problem," Dec said.

"So what are you up to? What's going on with that case Trevor Ross gave you?"

"Which one? Eden Ross or Dr. Devine?"

"Both," Ian said.

"Eden Ross finally contacted her father and she's all right. And my job with Dr. Devine is done. She had a stalker problem, but the Providence P.D. arrested the guy earlier this week. He confessed."

Ian stretched his legs out in front of himself and clasped his hands behind his head. "Sounds like you haven't had any problems staying celibate."

"Have you?" Dec asked.

Ian shook his head. "No problems. I mean, I have to tell you, it's tough. The more you try to keep from thinking about women, the more it seems to happen. But, when I'm feeling it, I just—relieve the pressure."

"That's important," Dec said. "In fact, I just heard that it's really medically necessary for a guy to do it every week or so. Did you know that?"

Ian gave him an odd look. "What the hell are you talking about?"

"Masturbation," Dec said.

"Well, don't talk about that! I don't wanna hear it. You're supposed to be thinking pure thoughts if you have any hope in hell of making it through this."

"Jaysus, Ian, sometimes you can be such a wanker."

Ian stood. "Come on. I've got an hour to kill. I know

a great pub just a few blocks from here. McSorley's. I'll buy you a pint. You know, we were supposed to get together every week and discuss this whole experience. I haven't heard one word from either you or Marky. Seems we're all pretty busy."

Dec nodded. "Maybe we should make plans," he offered, hoping that the idea would go nowhere.

"Yeah," Ian said. "I'll get back to you on that."

They walked out of the office together, but when they got to the receptionist desk, Celine called out to Dec. "Declan, I have Rachel Merrill on line two. She says it's important. Very important. She sounds a bit upset."

"Who is Rachel Merrill?" Ian asked.

"A client. Let me just go back and get this call. I'll meet you at McSorley's in a few minutes." Dec hurried back down the hall to his office and picked up the phone, punching in the button for line two.

"Rachel? Hi, it's Dec. What's up?"

"You have to help me." Her voice was barely above a whisper.

"What's wrong? Where are you?"

"I'm at home. Yesterday, someone keyed my car at the university. And then, today, I got home from lunch with Daniel Ellsworth to find my car covered in red paint." She drew a shaky breath. "The car was in my garage at my house. They just walked into the garage and threw paint everywhere." He heard a sob over the phone. "I'm scared, Dec. Should I call the police?"

"Are you in the house right now?"

"Yes."

"Can you turn on the security system?"

"It's not finished," she said. "They're waiting for some part that was missing."

Dec cursed, then raked his hand through his hair. "All right. It'll take me a few minutes to get there. Hang up and I'm going to call you back on my cell phone. I want you to stay on the line until I get to you." He grabbed his phone out of his pocket, then noticed the two missed messages from Rachel. He'd turned the phone off in a meeting earlier that afternoon and had forgotten to turn it back on. How long had she been locked inside her house, terrified?

"All right. Hang up now. I'll call you back just as soon as I get to my car," he said.

Dec headed back out to the lobby. He stopped at Celine's desk and asked her to call McSorley's and make his apologies to Ian. Then he shoved the glass doors open and headed to the elevator. As he was driving out of the parking ramp, he punched in the number for Rachel's home phone, then hit "send" the moment he got out on to the street.

She picked up the phone after the first ring. "Hi," she said.

"Tell me exactly what happened," he demanded.

"I told you. I just came home, opened the garage and saw my car. It was covered in clear red paint. It—it looks like blood. And there are words written on the back window." She took a ragged breath. "Die Bitch. Did they let him out of jail? Why would Jerry do this? They must be watching him, aren't they?"

"Rachel, Jerry is still in jail. He didn't have enough money to post bail."

"What does this mean?" she asked.

"I don't think Jerry Abler is the guy."

The other end of the line went silent. "Please hurry."

"I'll be there in just a few minutes," Dec said. "I want you to go upstairs and pack a bag. Keep talking to me, all right?"

Fifteen minutes later, Dec pulled into the driveway of Rachel's house and hopped out of the car. She met him at the back door, throwing her arms around his neck and holding on for dear life. "Come on, come on," he murmured, running his fingers through her hair. "It'll be all right. I'm here now. You're safe."

"I thought this was over," she said, trembling. "You said it was over."

"I thought it was. But we'll figure this out, I promise." He glanced around her kitchen. "Where's your bag?"

She pointed to her suitcase, sitting in the hallway to the foyer. "He must be watching me," she said. "He knows I'm back home. He's been at the university and at the station. He's everywhere now. He knows everything about me."

Dec crossed the kitchen and grabbed the bag, then took her hand. "Baby, he probably has known for a while. He's just getting bolder. You were out of town, he couldn't see you and he got mad. He wants you to know that you can't get away from him." Dec kissed her forehead. There was no way to reassure her, at least not until he got her out of this house and someplace where she'd feel safe. "Come on, let's go."

"Are we going back to Maine?"

"No, we're going to my place."

She nodded, pasting a tight smile on her face. "Your place. I'll be safe there."

Dec stepped outside and checked to make sure there was no one around, then led Rachel to his car. He tossed her bag into the backseat, then ran around to the driver's side and hopped in. As they pulled out of the driveway, he stared in the rearview mirror, watching for any traffic behind them. Then he grabbed up his phone and called the office. Celine picked up.

"Hey, it's Dec. I want you to get a hold of Davis and tell him I want that security system at the Merrill residence up and running by sunset tonight. I don't care if he has to charter a damn jet to go pick up the part, I want it done. Or his ass will be providing security for charity events in Antarctica."

He flipped the phone shut and shoved it back into his pants' pocket then glanced over at Rachel. She looked so vulnerable, her hands clutched in front of her, her face pale. He cursed himself for his part in all this. He should have suspected the arrest had come all to easily. Even Rachel hadn't believed they arrested the right guy.

"When we get back to my place, I'll make you some dinner and then you can curl up on the sofa and watch a movie." He forced a smile. "I have a big-screen television."

A tiny smile curved the corners of her mouth. "What is it with guys and their televisions?"

"I don't know. You tell me," Dec said, trying to draw her into a conversation. "I'm sure it's something sexual. Maybe instead of whipping out our dicks and measuring them, we just buy a big-screen TV instead. By the way, mine is fifty inches." He paused. "It's a plasma screen."

Rachel giggled at the joke and Dec reached across the back of her seat and furrowed his fingers into the hair at her nape, gently turning her toward him. "I'm going to like having you around again."

"If I didn't know any better, I'd say you put that paint on my car, just so you could break the four-day rule." She drew a shaky breath. "But I know better."

"Yeah, you do."

"Yesterday, I came out to the parking lot at the university to find that my car had been keyed. Scratched up one side and down the other. A really deep gouge."

"Why didn't you call me then?"

Her lower lip trembled as she fought back tears and she bit it in an attempt to keep her emotions under control.

"It's all right," Dec said. "I know you're scared, but this is good. He's coming out into the open. He'll be easier to catch."

"I thought I was being paranoid. I can't look at anyone the same anymore. Even Daniel and Simon."

"What about Daniel and Simon?"

Rachel took a deep breath. "Daniel admitted yesterday that, at one time, he'd hoped we might have a—a future. And he also said that he thought Simon had a crush on me."

"He what?" Dec cursed, a flood of jealousy nearly overwhelming him. "Is there any man who isn't in love with you? Rachel, these are motives here. You should have told me."

"I didn't know until yesterday," she insisted. "I mean, it was surprising, but we've been friends for years. I once had a little crush on him, too, but our timing was never right. Besides, he couldn't have done this. He was with me when it happened. And Simon was teaching classes all morning."

"You're sure of that?"

She nodded. "As far as I knew, Jerry Abler was the guy and he was in jail. I figured the scratch on my car was just some random vandalism. I called the campus police and they filled out a report. They said they'd take a look at the videotapes and see if they could figure out who did it."

"There are videotapes?" Dec asked, his interest suddenly sharpened.

"There are cameras all over campus. They all feed into campus security."

"All right. I'm going to call over there and make sure I get a chance to see the tapes. They might have missed something."

"Do you think he wants to kill me?" she asked.

She blurted out the question so quickly that he knew she really didn't want to hear the answer. Dec shook his head. "I don't think so. He wants your attention, that's all. And he's using the language he needs to get it. He wants you to be frightened because in some twisted way, he thinks it will bring you closer to him. It'll give him control over you."

Dec took her hand and wove his fingers through hers, then drew her wrist up to his lips. "Hey, I also have a really big whirlpool tub in my bathroom. I could make you a nice bubble bath when we get home."

"That would be nice," she said.

They passed the rest of the ride in silence, but Dec

knew Rachel's mind was going a mile a minute. He wanted to distract her, but until he could take her into his arms and kiss her, there was nothing he could do. He thought about pulling over and drawing her into his arms, but then realized it would be best to get her home first.

They drove around another fifteen minutes before Dec headed back to his house. He watched the street carefully, then pulled the BMW into the garage and closed the door behind them. He turned off the ignition, then immediately leaned over and took Rachel's face between his hands. "It'll be all right, baby. I promise." He kissed her gently and she seemed to melt into him, her fingers grabbing hold of the lapels of his suit jacket and holding him close.

He kept kissing her, softly playing at her mouth until she drew back. "All right?" he asked.

Rachel nodded.

Dec helped her out of the car, then grabbed her bag and showed her into the house. The cleaning lady had been there the day before, so he knew everything was tidier than it usually was. She followed him through the dim interior, her hand tucked in his. "The television is in the den," he said.

"I'm more interested in a hot bath."

"I can do that for you." He led her upstairs and showed her the bedroom. "Why don't you get undressed and I'll go start the bath."

"Stay with me," she said.

Dec cleared his throat, then nodded. "All right." Rachel began to remove her clothes as if in a trance, not really noticing that he was there at all. He opened her bag and found the silk robe she'd worn up at the cabin and when she was naked, he wrapped it around her, then gave her a hug. Any desire he had for her was now overwhelmed by a need to soothe and protect her. The woman standing before him wasn't the Rachel he knew. This was a woman who was terrified of what her life had become. And it had been partially his fault that it had gotten this bad.

They walked to the bathroom and Rachel sat on the edge of the tub while he filled it. He didn't have any bubble bath, so he dumped some liquid soap into the tub and it seemed to do the trick. When the tub was high enough, he turned off the taps and stepped back. "The button for the jets is right there. But with the bubbles, you probably shouldn't turn them on or you'll be buried." He paused. "I'll just leave you."

"You can stay," she said. "I don't really want to be alone right now."

"All right," he said.

"You can watch," she murmured. "Some men find voyeurism very exciting."

She said the words without her usual scholarly tone and Dec wondered if she even realized what she'd said. He sat down on the toilet and watched as she dropped her robe and stepped into the tub. She hesitated for a moment as her foot got used to the temperature of the water, then slowly put the other foot in and lowered herself into the bubbles.

God, she was beautiful, Dec thought. He wanted to capture that moment, the moment when she stood with her back to him, her arms held out at her sides, her fingers delicately extended. She looked like a painting by one of those French guys, with every curve of her body washed in a soft light, every detail just slightly blurred.

He held his breath as she arched back, her head resting on the edge of the tub, her breasts just breaking the surface of the water. Once again, Rachel had been right. Watching her was incredibly arousing, but even more so was the fact that he wasn't supposed to do any more than watch.

When he was around Rachel, nearly every thought in his head was sexual. It made him more aware of her as a woman, aware of the power she held over him. Dec released a tightly held breath and closed his eyes. This was pure torment and he was loving every minute of it.

RACHEL SANK DOWN INTO THE warm water, her eyes closed, the tension slowly seeping out of her body. This was exactly what she needed. How could Declan possibly have known that? How did he always seem to know what would make her feel safe or happy or relaxed? Though the connection between them was strong, it wasn't just sexual. They seemed to share a deeper understanding of each other.

Right now, she knew he was watching her. He wanted to touch her, not to seduce her, but to assure himself that she was all right. In the car, he couldn't seem to stop touching her and she was glad for it. At the moment, it had been all she needed to keep from dissolving into hysterical weeping.

Rachel opened her eyes and glanced over at him, only to find Dec sitting with his eyes closed and his brow furrowed into a frown. She hadn't noticed until now, but he seemed a little tense as well. "Would you like to join me?" she asked.

His eyes opened and he blinked. "What?"

Rachel held out a bubble-coated arm. "Come on. This is a big tub. I'm sure you know that two can fit."

"I've never had a woman in that tub," he said. "You're the first."

"I'm honored," Rachel teased. "But I'd be happier if you came in here with me."

"You sure?"

She nodded. Declan stood and walked over to the tub, then slowly shrugged out of his suit jacket, tossing it over the edge of the sink. Rachel watched him undo his tie, then unbutton his dress shirt. She hadn't realized how different he looked in a suit, older, serious, more conservative. Though she liked the look, it wasn't really the Declan she knew.

He stripped down to his boxer briefs, then stood watching her, his thumbs skimming beneath the waistband as if he hadn't thought twice about accepting her offer. And then, he shoved the boxers down, kicked out of them and stepped into the tub.

Dec winced at the heat of the water, but quickly grew accustomed to the temperature. He grabbed her hands and pulled her forward, then moved to sit behind her. Rachel settled back against him, her hips nestled between his legs.

"Wow," Dec murmured. "This is kinda nice. It's perfect for two."

Rachel closed her eyes and tipped her head back.

"Hmmm." She'd gone from the depths of fear to the heights of absolute calm in the course of an hour. This was exactly what she needed, the warm water swirling over her naked skin, a long-limbed man holding her against his body. It was the best kind of therapy for anything that ailed her.

"I guess I don't make much of a voyeur," he said. "I don't have the patience to just watch."

"You're not exactly supposed to be invited to watch," she said. "You're supposed to do it secretly. That's part of the thrill."

"Aren't voyeurs just Peeping Toms?"

"All Peeping Toms are voyeurs, but not all voyeurs are Peeping Toms. Some people get sexually aroused by watching. There's nothing wrong with that if it's done in a safe and legal environment. It's a well-recognized paraphilia."

Dec growled, then kissed her neck playfully. "I love it when you talk sex to me. But what's a paraphilia?"

"It's sexual arousal in response to objects or situations that don't have a possibility of reciprocal sexual activity. But it also refers to sexual practices out of the mainstream."

"Like what? Like getting dressed up in your girl-friend's skirts?"

"Yeah, if you're turned on by the clothes. Then there's fetishism, which is arousal from a body part, usually non-sexual. Like the foot. That's a popular one."

"I have a hard time with that one," Dec said. "I mean, my feet are stuck inside my shoes all day long. They're about as sexy as my earlobes."

"I think your earlobes are really sexy," Rachel said, glancing back at him. She reached beneath the water and grabbed his foot, then held it up. "This is a beautiful foot."

"But do you find it sexy?" he asked.

Rachel decided to try something she never had. She brushed the soap off his foot, then leaned forward and kissed his instep. Slowly running her tongue along the arch, she stopped when she reached the toes, drawing his big toe into her mouth and sucking it gently.

Dec's breath caught and for a moment, he stiffened, then let out a low groan. "Oh, fuck," he murmured.

"I think your feet are very sexy," she whispered as she continued to suck on each toe. She'd always read that men's feet were particularly sensitive to oral stimulation, but she'd never had the opportunity for any real-life research. From Dec's reaction, she knew that the research had been correct.

"See how this works," she said.

"Oh, yeah," he said. "You don't have to convince me."

Rachel giggled, then let his foot drop gently back down into the water. This time, when she leaned back, she felt his growing erection slide up along her spine. For such a swift and intense response, Dec must have enjoyed the toe sucking more than she'd anticipated.

"Now what?" he asked in a seductive voice. "Teach me more."

Rachel slowly rolled over until she faced him, her body still caught between his legs. "There's a lot of other things to explore if you're interested."

"What about your first date rule?" he asked, capturing her mouth for a quick kiss.

"I've been thinking that might be an arbitrary rule," she replied as she nuzzled his chest.

He bent down and grabbed her bottom lip between his teeth, giving it a gentle nip. "I completely agree. Especially if it's going to stand in the way of my education."

Rachel slowly rose and stood in front of him, running her palms over her soap-slicked skin, teasing at his desire. He watched her for a long time, his gaze moving up and down the length of her body. She stepped out of the tub and grabbed a towel from the rack, smiling as she walked out of the bathroom, the towel wrapped around her body.

Rachel wandered into Dec's bedroom. He'd set her bag in the doorway, but this time she knew his choice had been purposeful. He wanted her to share his bed. She tossed the bag on the bed and opened it, then pulled out a pair of summer pajamas she'd packed. The short-sleeved shirt and the little shorts had kittens all over the fabric and she dried off and slipped into them.

"Man, those are sexy."

Rachel glanced up to find Dec standing in the doorway to the bedroom, a towel wrapped around his waist. "You like them?" she asked.

"Better than Victoria's Secret any day." He ran his hands over his belly. "So, do you want something to eat?"

Rachel shook her head. "I'm fine. But I'm not sure I'm up for a movie."

"We have our date tomorrow night, we'll see one then."

"Our date," she said. In all the chaos of the afternoon, she'd forgotten about that. She'd missed her hair appointment and hadn't found anything to wear yet.

Dec pointed to the bed. "If you don't mind, I'm going to grab my pillow. I'll sleep on the sofa in the den."

"No," Rachel said, shaking her head. She crawled onto the mattress, rising on her knees as she raked her hands through her damp hair. "You'll sleep with me."

"All right," Dec said. She watched as he shifted on his feet, knowing what was going through his mind, making certain he knew it was an invitation and not an excuse. They both knew they couldn't spend an entire night in the same bed without touching and kissing. And that would lead to many more pleasures, pleasures neither one of them wanted to deny anymore.

She wanted to fall into bed with Dec right now, to strip off all his clothes and pull him on top of her. Losing herself in a haze of desire would be exactly what she needed, the touch of his body distracting her from all the other worries plaguing her mind. "Are you coming to bed?" she asked.

"In a few minutes," he replied. "I just want to call the office and have them go over and get those videotapes from university security. And then I'm going to send someone over to your house and see if they can pick up any evidence from the garage." He stepped up and slipped his arms around her waist, then gave her a slow, sensual kiss, his hands running over her body. When he'd had enough, he kissed her neck. "I'll be right back."

"I'll be waiting." She drew back the covers, then crawled beneath them. As she snuggled into his soft down pillows, Rachel smiled. Of all the places they'd lived together, she liked this one best.

She rolled over on her stomach and stared at the things

scattered on his nightstand. A bottle of vitamin C. A photo of Dec and five young children, Dec standing with his arms outstretched like the branches of a tree and the children swinging from them. A pile of change and a matchbook from a Providence night club. She picked up the matchbook and peeked inside, relieved to find it blank.

Curious, Rachel took her search a bit further and pulled out the drawer of his nightstand. It was filled with an assortment of small items, pens and pencils, a small flashlight, a bottle of aspirin. She pulled out a small black book and flipped through it, then saw that it was "his" black book. It was filled with phone numbers, each accompanied by the name of a girl. "Mandi M.," she murmured. "Tori K. Kari W."

Rachel had made an unofficial study of girls who had names that ended in "i" and she'd come to the conclusion that they were usually blonde, gorgeous and possessed a larger than average pair of breasts. She stared down at her own chest and sighed. She liked to think of herself as sexy, but next to girls like that, she paled in comparison.

Rachel set the black book back inside then pulled out a string of condoms. At least he was prepared, she mused. But had he put those in the nightstand just recently or did he keep a steady supply on hand? Rachel had never asked him about past girlfriends or lovers. In the beginning, it hadn't been any of her business and now, it didn't really matter. She was the woman in his bed, the woman he wanted here.

She closed the nightstand drawer and curled back up beneath the covers. Closing her eyes, she listened to the sounds of Dec moving around downstairs and she smiled. Once again, he'd made sure she was safe. As long as she was with him, nothing could hurt her.

THE HAND CAME OUT OF nowhere, clamping down on her mouth. Rachel tried to open her eyes. Maybe they were open and it was just so dark she couldn't see. No matter how hard she tried, she couldn't scream. The hand blocked whatever sound she tried to make.

Twisting against the grip, she fought frantically for air, but it was no use. She felt herself blacking out and rather than experiencing a sense of release, her panic only increased. This was how she was going to die, suffocated, second by second, losing her grip on life. She'd nearly resigned herself to her fate, ready to let go.

And then suddenly, the hand was gone. Rachel bolted upright and gasped for breath, her heart slamming in her chest. He was there beside her and with a soft cry, she scrambled across the bed to get away.

He reached out and grabbed her hand. "Hey," he said softly. "It's all right. You were having a bad dream."

The soft light from the hallway illuminated his silhouette and for a moment, Rachel thought the panic would overwhelm her. But then she recognized Declan and her pulse began to slow. Emotion surged inside her and she fought back a wave of tears. These wide swings between utter fear and blissful safety were beginning to wear her down.

Dec drew her into his arms and pulled her back down to lie beside him, gently stroking her back and kissing her face. "Better now?" he asked.

She nodded, nuzzling into his warm, naked chest. Rachel lay there for a long time, listening to the strong rhythm of his heart and letting his strength seep into her. She wanted this closeness. In truth, she needed to feel closer.

Pushing up on her elbow, she stared down into his face, the features just visible in the dim light. He watched her silently and without thinking, she crawled on top of him and began to move. Her hips rocked up and down against his crotch and Dec moaned, arching into her body as if inviting her to continue.

There was no conscious decision to seduce him, just an unspoken agreement that this was the time and place. She felt it, in her soul and deep inside her body, an undeniable need to ease the ache there. She had to have him—now, not later. Bending forward, Rachel slid down over his hips, moving lower and lower until she straddled his thighs.

He was already hard, the outline of his erection evident beneath the soft cotton of his boxer briefs. Rachel rubbed her hand back and forth over the ridge and Dec moaned, twisting beneath her touch. His eyes were closed and she knew he'd have a hard time fighting the pleasure she was giving him.

She pulled the waistband of his boxers down to reveal his hard cock. Wrapping her fingers around it, she slowly began to stroke him. But it wasn't enough to just touch him, she needed to taste him as well. Taking the tip into her mouth, Rachel flicked her tongue over the head of his penis. She seemed to connect with all the right nerves because Dec jerked beneath her, then moaned again, softly whispering her name.

She took her time pleasing him with her mouth and he grew even harder, his erection straining against her hand. Rachel grabbed the boxer briefs and pulled them off, sliding down with them until she reached his feet.

Grabbing his foot, she pressed a kiss into the curve of his instep, then moved to his toes. But when she took his little toe into her mouth and began to suck, Dec pulled his foot away. "If you do that, I'll come right now," he warned her.

Rachel laughed softly, then crawled back on top of him. "Have I discovered a weakness?"

He reached up and brushed the hair away from her face, groaning as he tugged her head back. "You're my weakness," he said, his voice ragged.

Bending toward him, Rachel kissed him, lingering over his mouth the way she lingered over his penis. "I need you," she murmured. "I need to feel you inside of me."

Dec smoothed his hand over her cheek, turning her face until he could see it more clearly in the dim light. "Are you awake?" he asked.

Rachel nodded. "Yes. I know what I'm doing."

"Are you doing this because you're afraid and you want me to make you feel safe?"

"I'm doing this because I want you," she replied. "Nothing more."

Dec pulled her back down into another deep kiss, his mouth capturing hers, plundering hers with his tongue. "I want you, too," he said, a desperate edge to his voice. "God, I want you so much it scares me."

Rachel reached for the hem of her pajama top and tugged it over her head, then tossed it on the floor. She'd always let her partner take the lead in the past, believing that men gained more pleasure from controlling their partner in sex. But tonight, she felt as if this was her awakening, a time to take what she needed.

Dec reached up and cupped her breasts in his hands, teasing at the nipples until they were hard peaks. They'd waited so long for this that she'd expected this moment to be frantic and wild. But instead it was quiet and gentle, two people intent on savoring every sensation.

Rachel slid her legs along his, until she lay on top of him. His penis pressed against her belly and she rubbed against it, rising up every now and then before dropping down again. Though it was such a simple act, it made Dec even more aroused and he clutched at her backside, urging her to move at his direction.

"I'm so close," he said. "From the minute you touched me, I felt like I was nearly there."

Rachel smiled. "I'm glad I have that effect on you."

"Oh, you do," he murmured. He reached down and slid his hands beneath her boy shorts, bunching the lacy trim in his fists, then slowly worked them down her legs. A few moments, later, they joined his boxer briefs on the floor.

The feel of their naked bodies stretched out together set every nerve in Rachel's body tingling. His hands skimmed over her backside, then up to her shoulders and back again as he kissed her. It was good that they'd waited, Rachel mused. Though it might have been a wonderful physical release a few days ago, Rachel felt as if they'd somehow grown closer since then.

She brought her knees back up around his hips, letting his cock nestle between her legs. And then, she drew forward and he was probing at her entrance. Rachel held her breath, enjoying the feel of him nearly inside of her.

"Oh, God," he murmured. "Don't do that to me."

But Rachel didn't listen. She slowly lifted herself up on her knees, then sank down on top of him. He slid inside her, inch by inch, but before she could bury him completely, Dec grabbed her hips and stopped. "We should use a condom," he said.

"Umm," Rachel murmured, her mind focused on the feel of him inside of her. "All right. That would be good."

Dec gently lifted her up, then twisted beneath her to grab a condom from the bedside table. He struggled to tear open the plastic packet and when it finally did, he gave it to her to smooth over his stiff shaft.

"Now?" she murmured, crawling back on top of him.

Dec groaned, pressing at the damp spot between her legs. "Now."

This time, she came down all the way, until he was buried deep inside of her. Rachel sighed and then smiled. She'd imagined how this might feel, but it was so much better. He was thick and hard and he filled her completely, his warmth, his strength, his courage.

She began to move above him, drawing him in and out of her body in a slow and easy rhythm. Dec watched her, his gaze fixed on her face, his expression intense. But what began quietly, soon turned into something much more desperate and passionate.

As Dec's pleasure began to increase, he grabbed her waist and flipped her beneath him. Bracing his arms on either side of her, he continued to move but now he controlled the tempo and Rachel found herself losing touch with reality.

Through a hazy desire, she watched his face, tense in an attempt to maintain control, the clenched jaw, the closed eyes, the focused expression. But she didn't care. She wanted him to lose control, to give it up to her in the same way she'd made herself vulnerable to him.

He drove into her hard again and again, then stopped, leaning over her and kissing her deeply. "You're making me crazy," he said. "I want you too much." He slid down on her body until he could catch his arms beneath her legs, then began to kiss her belly.

A moment later, his mouth was on her, his tongue teasing at her clitoris. Rachel knew the feeling, knew how intense the orgasm would be and how quickly it would come. But this time, she wouldn't give in to it. She'd wait and share it with Dec.

He brought her close again and again and she fought the pleasure. And when she could fight it no more, Rachel put her hands in his hair and tugged him back up along her body. "I want you inside me when I come," she said.

He filled her again, still as hard as he was before, and began to move. But this time, Rachel let go, surrendering to the wild sensations that coursed through her body. She wasn't sure it would happen, but as he increased his tempo, she felt herself spiraling upward. There was no stopping it and Rachel shifted beneath him, finding just the right spot to bring her the rest of the way.

Her orgasm hit her like a surge of electricity, gripping every nerve in her body for just one unbearable second.

And then Rachel tumbled forward, falling into it, the rush of pleasure, the shocking spasms and the overwhelming satisfaction.

She hadn't realized that Dec had found his release at the same time until her mind regained some sense of reality again. He was gasping for breath, driving into her, and Rachel sighed, running her hands over his chest.

There had been nothing bizarre or kinky about it. It was perfectly normal sex. But at the same time, it was the most extraordinary sex she'd ever experienced. Because it was with a man who touched her heart and her soul. She was falling in love with Declan Quinn and there was nothing she could do about it.

8

DEC STARED DOWN AT the pile of magazines that Rachel had handed him, his mouth hanging open. "What the hell are you doing with all this porn in your office?"

"We used it for a study," Rachel said, her eyes fixed on the book she was reading. "I couldn't throw it away since we bought it with grant money. Besides, those magazines don't really go out of date that fast. They're all pictures."

"You realize what you're asking me to do?" Dec said.

Rachel glanced up from her book, sending him an exasperated expression. "How am I supposed to get any work done if you insist on talking to me the whole time? I have things to do and since you're determined to accompany me everywhere I go, then you need something to occupy yourself."

"So you decided porn would do the trick? That titty magazines would occupy me?"

"Don't tell me you don't like porn," she said.

"Well, I do occasionally indulge, but it's not a huge part of my life."

"I'm giving you permission to indulge, so just sit back and enjoy it. I've got at least another hour's worth of work to do and then we can go."

Dec sat back on Rachel's leather sofa and picked through the selection of magazines. There were all sorts, from the standard men's magazines to some pretty raunchy stuff. "What exactly were you studying?" he asked.

"We asked men ages eighteen to thirty-five to choose their fantasy female from the magazine. And then we took the qualities of those women, quantified them and ran them through a computer program to see if there was a typical fantasy object for most American men of that demographic."

"So you sat around and looked at porn with these guys?"

"No," Rachel said. "They sat in a room and went through the magazines. They picked out a girl, then brought it out to me or one of my assistants and we logged it into the book."

"You put a guy in a room alone with a bunch of porn?"

"We asked that they refrain from pleasuring themselves with our porn, but I didn't ask what they planned to do once they left. I'm studying sexual behaviors, Dec. It would be hypocritical to begrudge them their own pleasures."

Dec flipped through one of the magazines. "So what did you find out?"

Rachel closed the book in front of her and set it aside. "There was a certain type of woman who appealed to the majority of the men. After we made a composite photo, we gave it back to the men in our study and asked them on a scale of one to ten, how they'd rate the woman as their ultimate fantasy. She scored an 8.7, which was statistically significant."

"And what does that mean?"

"We postulated that society, through media images in television, movies and magazines, trains men to be attracted to a certain type of woman. Back in the caveman days, these women were sturdy, strong, good gatherers and able to bear plenty of children. And this held true up until the industrial revolution. But now, things are changing. Men don't take into account how a woman will help extend his genetic line. He's simply interested in the sexiest fuck on the planet." She smiled. "Excuse my Latin."

Dec frowned. "Is that true?"

"Our research proved that. Once a woman was freed from the difficult and dangerous work of keeping a home and bearing children, she was free to be something else—a sexual object. A woman could be incapable of sustaining marriage and a family, yet the strongest men will choose her because she has large breasts and a tight ass." She frowned. "As you can see, this doesn't bode well for the future of mankind."

Dec chuckled at her sarcastic delivery of the last line. "I love listening to you when you get all academic on me."

Rachel continued her work as Dec paged through the magazines. He found his mind not captured by the sexy images he saw, but by what he and Rachel had shared the previous night. Though he had been guilty in the past of choosing women because of their looks, with Rachel it was different. Not that she wasn't the most beautiful woman on the planet, but he was attracted to her because of her intelligence, her vulnerability and her honesty.

And then there was the way she made him feel in bed. He wasn't sure what it was and maybe it was a combination of all the things he loved about her, but when she turned her full attention to making him feel good, there was nothing like it in the world. Every touch, every movement, drove him wild with desire.

He drew a deep breath, the thoughts in his head spinning into further fantasies. He had been in a constant state of arousal since the very moment he'd met Rachel and until last night, there'd been no decent relief. But now, he had every belief that what they'd shared would be enjoyed again.

With a satisfied smile, Dec picked up another magazine and flipped to the centerfold. He held it up, letting the page open into his lap. "Look at this," he said, turning the magazine so Rachel could see. "You have much nicer breasts than this woman. See, these don't look real. Yours look…natural."

"Thank you," Rachel said.

"And you have nicer hair," Dec added. "I like your hair. It's…different."

"Different good or different bad?"

"Good," Dec said. He plucked at his own hair. "It's wavy and thick, so I can sink my fingers into it when I'm kissing you. I like that."

"Anything else?" Rachel asked, a smile twitching at the corners of her mouth.

"If I had to describe my fantasy woman, she'd look pretty much like you." He paused. "Well, she'd look exactly like you." He tossed the magazine aside and stood, then crossed the office to her. Leaning forward, his hands braced on her desk, he kissed her upturned face, first her cheeks, then her nose, then her mouth.

"Do I have to give you something else to occupy your time?" she asked. "I have some nice drawings of sexual positions you might like."

"I'll let you know if I need them for reference." He circled around the desk and pulled her to her feet, then wrapped his arms around her waist. This time, he gave her a long, deep kiss, designed solely to make her forget her work and turn her attention back to him.

"You know pretty much everything about sex, don't you," he murmured, his voice warm against her ear. She nodded. "There's one thing you don't know, though."

"What's that?" Rachel asked.

"Never give a man porn when he's locked in an office with a beautiful woman."

"We're not locked in," she said.

"Then I think you better lock us in," Dec countered.

Rachel slowly backed away from him. At first, he thought she'd find an excuse to put him off. He turned around and leaned against the edge of her desk. And when he heard the lock click, he smiled.

The click was like a starter's pistol and Dec walked across the office and grabbed Rachel, dragging her into a frantic kiss. He didn't want to spend time with preliminaries. They could do that in the privacy of his apartment later that night. Right now, he just had to have her naked body in his arms.

His hands fumbled with her clothes, stripping them off as quickly as he could. At first, Rachel seemed surprised by his aggression, but then she laughed softly and began to tear at his clothes, too.

Within seconds, they were both naked, their mouths

still fixed on each other's. He couldn't get enough of her as his hands skimmed over her body, enjoying each sexy curve. Every inch of her skin was so soft and warm, like silk against his fingertips.

Dec reached down and grabbed her behind her thighs, then picked her up and wrapped her legs around his waist. If last night had been slow and easy, then this would be the exact opposite. He wanted it all and he wanted it right away. He pressed her back against the bookcases and Rachel spread her arms out and held on to the shelves for balance.

"God, you feel so good," he whispered, his body pressed into hers. He reached down and cupped her breast in his hand, then bent to capture her nipple, licking and sucking until it was hard.

Rachel groaned, arching against him. "Oh, yes." She let go of the shelf and wrapped her arms around his head. "Oh my." She rocked against him, his cock sliding against her clitoris. He moved with her, growing slick with the damp of her desire.

Dec shifted, grasping her buttocks and moving her up and down against him. Her breath came in quick gasps and she moaned in rhythm to his thrusts. "Do you want it?" he asked, his tone thick with desperation. "Do you want me inside you?"

"Yes," she replied. "Now. Please."

"Condom," he murmured. Wrapping her legs more tightly around his waist he walked with her to the desk where his jeans hung off the edge. He set her down on the smooth wood surface, then grabbed his wallet and pulled out the plastic packet he'd tucked inside. He tore it open, fumbling with the slippery rubber before he smoothed it over his cock.

He picked her up again but Dec wasn't sure he could hold her and come at the same time, so he shoved the papers off her desk and laid her back down in front of him. She seemed ready for him, but Dec wasn't about to ignore her needs. He spread her legs, then knelt down to lick and tease at her clitoris.

She was already aroused and within a minute or two, she cried out, exploding in a powerful orgasm. He wanted to feel the spasms of her body so he quickly rose and slipped inside her. She was hot and swollen and still convulsing as he began to move inside her.

It didn't take long before he was dancing on the edge of his own orgasm. Dec gathered himself, pushing back against the pleasure until it was too much to bear, then pushing back again. He grabbed her foot and brought it up to his mouth, kissing her instep, then running his tongue up to her toes.

How could it feel this good? Even the very first time he came inside a woman, it hadn't felt this good. It wasn't just the physical pleasure that he was experiencing but the sensation of possessing Rachel, of her being entirely his for the time he was inside her.

He'd never been a jealous person, but he knew now how a man might become crazy with need for a woman. If anyone ever dared try to take Rachel from him, there'd be no limit to what he'd do to keep her. It wasn't a rational thought, Dec knew that. But the feelings inside of him were so powerful that he felt he couldn't control them.

He brought her legs over his shoulders, then stared

down into her face, her beautiful face. Her eyes were closed, her damp lips parted. She was his fantasy come to life. Though he'd said the words to her, he didn't really know what they meant until now. This was all he'd ever needed or wanted.

Dec reached down and slid his thumb gently between their bodies, rubbing at her again. After last night, after the sensation of her body clenching around him, he wanted be inside her when she came. He moved slowly, giving her time to relax and recover from her first orgasm. But it wasn't long before she began rocking against him in an ever-quickening rhythm.

He was close but Dec waited, holding back far longer than he'd ever thought possible. And when Rachel arched against him, he let go, joining her in a shattering orgasm that seemed to last forever, driving into her one last time.

Spent, Dec fell forward. He nuzzled her neck, kissing a trail from her ear to her shoulder, then back again. "I bet none of your research subjects ever had that reaction to those magazines," he murmured.

Rachel laughed softly, then grabbed his hair and pulled his head up so she could look at his face. She gave him a slow, deep kiss, then sighed. "Remind me to put those in a bag so we can take them home."

"I don't need pictures of naked women to get me going," Dec said. "You do that just fine on your own."

She sighed, then pulled him back down on top of her. "I don't think I want the police to catch my stalker. Then you could be with me forever and make me feel like this all the time."

Dec wrapped his arms around her and hugged her tight. Funny, he was thinking exactly the same thing.

RACHEL STOOD STARING INTO HER suitcase and studied her wardrobe possibilities, searching for an outfit that was sophisticated, yet simple, and flattered her figure as well.

She and Dec had come back to his place from her office and immediately tumbled into his bed, repeating the experiences of that afternoon. She'd just assumed that they'd stay in bed until it was time for her to leave for her shift at the station, but Dec was determined that they go out on their date.

He'd already made a reservation for dinner and though they'd missed going to an early movie, Rachel agreed that a night out would be good for them. After all, an entire day of sex had left her famished—and a bit exhausted. And if they stayed in Dec's bed any longer, she wasn't sure she'd be able to get out.

"Are you ready?" he asked.

"No," she called. "I'm not sure what to wear."

"Don't worry," he said. "You'll look pretty in anything you put on."

For most men, the compliment would have simply been a way to move things along a little faster. But Rachel honestly believed that Dec would be attracted to her whether she wore a potato sack or a designer gown.

She plucked a black camisole from the suitcase and set it aside, then found a pretty black peasant skirt, adorned with jet beads. She usually wore the camisole underneath another blouse, but she decided to be daring tonight. Dropping her robe, Rachel pulled the camisole over her head, not bothering with a bra.

The hem rested just above her belly button and the skirt, just below, offering a tempting view of her stomach. She turned around in front of the full-length mirror on the back of Dec's bedroom door, then smiled. It was simple and very sexy. She grabbed a cropped jacket to put on when she reached the station, then slipped into a pair of strappy sandals.

"I'm ready," she called as she walked out the bedroom door.

Dec was waiting outside the room, his shoulder braced against the wall. When he saw her, he straightened, then smiled. "Wow," he said. His gaze slowly raked her body. "You're not wearing any underwear, are you?"

Rachel smiled. "Is that a problem?"

"I'll let you know," he said. He grabbed her hand and pulled her along, through the kitchen door. When they got outside, Dec helped her into his car then circled around to get behind the wheel. He started the car and popped in a CD. Soft jazz filled the car.

Rachel sat back in the leather seat and smiled. Of all the things they'd done together, this was the most normal. It was as if they were just a regular couple going out on a Saturday night. She turned to Declan and smiled. She'd met him not even a week ago and yet it seemed as if they'd known each other for ages. The details of their lives before they met weren't important. Yet, Rachel still wanted to know more about the man she was falling for.

"I guess that whole celibacy promise is down the drain," she said. "What will your brothers say?"

"I don't know. I'll definitely have to pay up. And I guess I'll get razzed for it for the next few years." He glanced over at her. "But it was well worth it."

"Did you learn anything?"

"Yeah, I think I did."

"And what is that?"

He paused, as if to consider his words carefully. "I think when I decided to propose the bet, I was hoping it might change something in me. That if I wasn't constantly looking for sex, maybe I'd be able to see something more in a woman."

"Like what?"

"Like a future," he said. "Something that lasts longer than just a few nights in bed. Other guys have it and I guess I wanted it, too."

"And is that what your brothers want?" Rachel asked, steering the conversation in a different direction.

Dec shrugged. "I think so. We had kind of a screwy childhood and I think that made it more difficult for us to form attachments. You could probably figure it all out for us."

"What happened?" Rachel asked.

"My ma got sick and me and my brothers were sent to Ireland to live with our grandmother."

"That must have been interesting," Rachel said.

"It probably would have been, if we hadn't stayed for eight years. Hell, almost nine. One day we had a family—parents, brothers and sisters, and a home—and the next day, we were on a plane going to live with a woman we'd never met. My mother's illness pretty much ruined the family financially so it was probably the only thing they could do. My grandmother was rich, we were poor." He looked over at her. "So, am I totally screwed up for the rest of my life? Or is there hope for me?"

"There are probably some scars, buried pretty deep," Rachel responded. "And I'd guess that you've maintained a distance with women, and with people in general, because you're afraid of being abandoned again. But you're an adult, Dec. You can look at those fears and face them for what they are. A lot of people have difficult childhoods but they get beyond them."

"I think that may be happening," he murmured.

Rachel wanted to ask him what he meant, but when she looked over at him, he seemed completely lost in his thoughts. Had she changed him somehow? Had their relationship made him realize it was possible to have a future with a woman? She drew a deep breath. And was she that woman?

So many times over the past week, she'd had to remind herself not to get caught up in the romance of it all. This was every woman's fantasy—handsome man come to rescue her, an undeniable chemistry, and then sex like she'd never had it before. Already, they'd shared so much and it was still early in their friendship.

There were so many different ways it could all turn out, she mused. They could continue on for a long time until the passion was spent, the interest faded. Or they could burn out quickly, unable to find anything more than sexual attraction. Or, they could spend the rest of their lives together.

Rachel knew the odds of making it to happily-ever-after weren't very good. But they did increase a bit considering how well she and Dec seemed to get along. She liked him. He was sweet and sexy and funny. And he was a man who enjoyed pleasing a woman. And not just in bed, but everywhere else, from opening her car door, to drawing her a bath, to bringing her breakfast in bed. He liked to make her smile and she'd grown to love him for that.

She sucked in a sharp breath, turning her gaze to the window. Love. She loved him. Or did she? This could be simply infatuation, the flood of affection that came with a new relationship. She'd have to be careful. Dec had his own demons to wrestle with when it came to love. Confiding her own feelings to him too early might just scare him away.

"Where are we going to dinner?" she asked.

"It's a surprise," he replied. "Oh, by the way, there's a box in the backseat. Can you reach around and get it for me?"

Rachel leaned between the two front seats and grabbed the small white box. "What is it?"

"It's for you," he said.

She laughed. "For me?"

"Since this was an official date, I figured I ought to give you something to remember it by. Go ahead, open it up."

"When did you have time to buy me something?"

"I made a few phone calls and then sent one of my guys out to pick it up."

She pulled the cover off the box and sighed. Tucked inside pretty pink tissue paper was a tiny bouquet of flowers, a nosegay. "In Victorian times, men used to give little bouquets like these to a woman they wanted to court," she said.

"I know," he said.

"How do you know that?" Rachel asked.

"I'm not a complete idiot in the romance department," he said. "My grandmother had a huge flower garden and she used to make us help her pick weeds. She used to rattle on about tussie-mussies and what all the different flowers meant. My brothers and I would just roll our eyes. I guess some of it must have stuck."

"Do you know what these mean?" she asked.

Dec examined the bouquet as she held it out to him. "The red roses are for passion. The forget-me-nots speak for themselves. The lavender is…devotion, I think. And the ferns are fascination."

Rachel held it up to her nose and drew in a deep breath. "You surprise me," she said.

"That's good, right?"

She leaned over the center console and gave him a quick kiss on the cheek. "Yes, that's very good."

They rode for a time in silence. Dec reached out and grabbed her hand, then brought it to his lips. "I'm looking forward to tonight," he said. "It's our first official date."

"It is," Rachel said. "I'm actually kind of nervous."

"Don't be," Dec teased. "I promise, I won't try to kiss you at the end of the evening. And I definitely won't ask if I can come in for a drink."

"Good," she said. "Because you should know, I'm not that kind of girl."

"No, you're definitely not that kind of girl," Dec said.

Rachel's cell phone rang and she picked up her purse, then set it back down. "No," she said. "No calls tonight."

"You should check to see who it is," Dec said.

She reached in her purse and glanced down at the caller I.D. The lighted display showed a number from the university exchange. She put the phone back, but then decided she ought to take it. "I promise I'll make it quick," she said, flipping it open. "Rachel Merrill."

"Professor Merrill, this is Officer Franklin from university security. I'm afraid we have some bad news for you."

Rachel glanced over at Dec and forced a smile. "Yes?"

"Someone has broken into your office and vandalized it."

"I see," Rachel said, trying to keep her voice calm. "Can you give me more details?" She listened as the officer relayed the damage and the method of break-in. "And what would you like me to do?"

"We'd like you to come down and see if there's anything missing. We've called the police because we understand you've been having trouble with a stalker. They're going to be sending a detective down. Can you meet him in a half-hour?"

Rachel drew in a deep breath. "I really don't think so. This will have to wait until tomorrow morning. I'm sure you can take care of it on your own."

"But, Professor Mer—"

She snapped the phone shut and tucked it back into her purse. "Sorry. Just some university business."

"Everything okay?" Dec asked.

She nodded. They drove on, Rachel mulling over the news she'd received and attempting to act as if it hadn't bothered her. The stalker was getting much more bold and aggressive and yet the police seemed no closer to finding out who it was. Even Dec had been stymied.

Detailed examination of the security tapes from the parking lot hadn't shown any hint of the person who vandalized her car. Either the stalker knew where all the cameras were and avoided them, or he was just downright lucky.

They were nearly downtown when Dec's cell phone rang. He reached into his jacket pocket and grabbed it, but she reached out and took it away from him. "Don't," she murmured.

"It's the office," he said. "I promise to make it quick. They might have something on your case."

The moment he flipped the phone open, Rachel knew what the call was about. Of course he'd find out about the vandalism. The university police had called the Providence police and they would have called his office. And his office would call him.

She listened to his side of the conversation as she stared out the window, knowing what would come next. When he stopped speaking, she risked a glance over at him to find his mouth set in a tight line.

"So you weren't planning to tell me what your call was all about?"

"I didn't want to spoil our date," Rachel said.

He cursed softly, shaking his head. "You didn't think I'd find out?"

"I didn't really think about it. I—I'm sorry. I should have said something, but I didn't want to ruin this."

"Baby, we can have as many dates as you want. But this is your safety we're talking about. That is number one. If you're not with me on that, then we have a serious problem."

"I didn't want tonight to be about you doing your job," she snapped. "I'm tired of that. I just wanted to have a nice night, just the two of us."

Dec glanced over his shoulder and pulled across a lane of traffic before guiding the car into an empty parking spot. He turned off the ignition and then faced her. "This stopped being about the job a while ago, Rachel. You have to know that. And maybe that's the problem. Maybe I've been spending too much time thinking about you and not enough time thinking about your stalker."

"No," she said, reaching out to touch his cheek. "No, you're the only one who has kept me together through all of this. I don't know what I would have done without you."

"Rachel, my first priority has to be your safety. And I honestly can't say that it has been. I didn't have to stay with you. I could have sent you somewhere safe or put an army of my guys around you."

"You can't leave me," she said, hearing a desperate edge to her voice. "I'm not sure I could feel safe without you."

He closed his eyes and sighed. "We're going over to the university. And we're going to figure out who is doing this."

"All right," she said. "Maybe there will be a clue there. Maybe there's a witness who saw something. We can figure this out." But even as she said the words, Rachel had her doubts. Her stalker had pretty much gone unnoticed for the past few months, slipping in and out of her life as if he knew her every move. They weren't any closer now than they had ever been.

She held the tiny bouquet up to her nose and inhaled

the scent of the flowers, closing her eyes. This couldn't go on forever. Sooner or later there would be a confrontation and whoever was doing this would reveal himself. And then she'd find out whether Dec would ever be a more permanent part of her life.

DEC WATCHED RACHEL THROUGH the glass window of the control booth, standing in the shadows so she couldn't see him. She was aware that he was there though. Since her show had gone on the air, she'd constantly glanced up to reassure herself. But with each glance, Dec felt more guilty.

He knew from the start he was breaking every professional rule he'd ever laid out for himself. Every instinct had told him to maintain his distance, to keep an objectivity with Rachel until her case was resolved. But he hadn't listened to his instincts, or at least not his professional instincts. He'd let his desire lead the way. And Rachel's stalker had continued on without consequence.

A knock sounded on the control room door and Rachel's producer turned as a skinny young man walked inside. He carried a package, wrapped in brown paper, and a stack of letters. "This is Dr. Devine's fan mail," he said. "And a package that came for her this morning."

"I'll take that," Dec said.

The young man handed him the mail, then stood awkwardly in front of Dec, shifting from foot to foot. "Are you watching over Dr. Devine?" he asked.

Dec nodded.

He reached into his back pocket and withdrew another envelope. "Would you give this to her? It's an apology note. I know it probably won't help, but I want her to have it."

"You're Jerry," Dec said.

The young man nodded. "The infamous Jerry," he said with a weak laugh. "Tell her I'm sorry I screwed things up."

"Why did you confess to something you hadn't done?"

He shrugged. "I don't know. I guess I thought people would look at me differently. Nobody ever sees me around here. I just bring the mail in and clean up the studios and make coffee. Nobody really cares what I do. But for a little while, they knew who I was."

"You shouldn't have confessed," Dec said.

"I know. After I did it, I couldn't take it back. The cops wouldn't listen. They didn't believe me, that I made it up. I knew too many details, they said. But I only knew those things because everyone at the station was talking about Dr. Devine's stalker."

Dec nodded. "I'll give her the letter."

The young man smiled, then nodded, backing out of the control room. "Thanks. I really appreciate that."

"I'm surprised the station let that guy come back," Dec muttered after Jerry was gone.

"He's the owner's nephew," Rachel's producer said.

Dec groaned. "Yeah, well, he should have known better." He turned his attention to Rachel's mail, flipping through the envelopes. They'd all been opened. Perhaps it was station policy or maybe security was looking for more letters from her stalker, but as he read through a few, Dec didn't find anything of interest.

Then he turned his attention to the package, flipping

it over. The moment he did, his heart stopped. A slash of red paint covered the brown paper, the same shade that had been tossed on Rachel's car.

He excused himself from the control room and walked across the hall to a small conference room. He set the package on the table. There was no telling what was inside. The prudent thing to do would be to call in the bomb squad.

He picked up the package and carried it through the hallway to the back door of the station. When he'd reached the middle of the empty parking lot, Dec knelt down and carefully began to unfasten the tape and string that held it together. He'd had some training in disarming explosives when he was in the navy, but if there was some type of explosive device inside, it probably wasn't as sophisticated as what he was used to dealing with.

He got the brown paper off the box without incident, then ran his finger under the lid of the shoebox. There weren't any trips or triggers, so he carefully tipped the box over and lifted the bottom off the top.

A small can of paint, streaked with dribbles of red, tumbled out. Stuck to it with a piece of tape was a note. Dec picked it up and squinted to read it by the parking lot lights. *I'm watching you,* the note said. *We'll talk soon.*

"Damn it," Dec muttered. He raked his hand through his hair, then carefully put the can of red paint back into the box. His first thought was to turn it over to the police. But maybe it was better to first give it to one of the private labs he used, just to make sure nothing was missed.

He walked over to his car and unlocked the truck, then put the box, along with the paper wrapping inside.

He wouldn't tell Rachel about this. It would only worry her further. But he did want to talk to Jerry. It seemed a bit more than coincidence that he was the one delivering the package.

Dec pressed the security buzzer for the back door and a few moments later the station guard came and let him in. He walked back toward Rachel's studio, searching for Jerry along the way. He found the guy in the coffee room, refilling the sugar and creamer dispensers.

"Hey," Dec said. "I need to talk to you."

Jerry glanced up. "Did I do something wrong?"

"That package you brought in. Where did you get it? It didn't come through the mail. There was no postage on it."

"Some lady dropped it off this morning."

"She brought it in?"

Jerry shook his head. "Yeah," he said. "I mean, no. She was out in the parking lot and I was coming into work. She asked if I'd deliver it to Dr. Devine. I said yes."

"And you didn't think anything of it? You know that Dr. Devine has a stalker."

"But this was a lady," Jerry said. "Dr. Devine's stalker is a man."

"We don't know that." Dec sighed. "What can you tell me about her? Describe her."

"I don't know," Jerry said. "She wasn't old. But she wasn't really young either. And she had kinda dark hair, but you couldn't really see because she was wearing a big hat. And sunglasses."

"How tall? As tall as Dr. Devine? And older or younger than Dr. Devine?"

"She was a little older I guess and about the same

height," he said. "She had a pretty good body. I noticed when she was walking back to her car."

"You saw her car?" Dec asked, stepping closer.

Jerry backed away. "Yeah. It was grey or maybe light blue. Some kind of sedan."

"What make and model?" Dec asked.

"Hey, I don't know much about cars. I couldn't tell you. But it didn't have four doors, only two. It was a little smaller, so maybe it was a foreign make."

"Anything else you can remember?"

Jerry thought about it for a while, then shrugged. "She was really nice to me," he offered.

"All right," Dec said. "I want you to keep this between me and you. Don't tell anyone else. Do I have your promise on that? I'm going to call someone from my firm over to see if you can pick out a photo of the type of car it was, or maybe make a drawing. Will you do that?"

"Only if you promise to give Dr. Devine that letter," Jerry said.

"All right. But I'm going to read it first."

A flush crept up the young man's cheeks. "Sure. I guess."

Dec made a quick phone call to the investigator he'd assigned to Rachel's case, then turned and walked back to the control room. He slipped through the door and took a seat in the shadows again. Rachel's voice came over the station speakers as she explained the proper and improper ways for men to masturbate. Dec hadn't realized there was an improper way, but then he learned something new from Rachel every day.

Finally, he had something new to offer her. Her

stalker wasn't a man, but a woman. His buddy at the FBI had been right all along. So that seriously cut down on the number of suspects they were looking at.

This woman had struck at the university, at the radio station and at Rachel's home. There had to be a way to connect all these dots, Dec mused. Somehow, he sensed that if he'd been working on the case full time and not spending his time protecting Rachel, he'd have been able to work this out. But his mind had been completely distracted by her.

The best thing to do would be to put a different detail on her, give her another bodyguard so he could go back to doing what he did best—investigating. But the thought of putting Rachel into someone else's care, even one of his own guys', wasn't really an option.

For now, he'd have to do both jobs, starting with a thorough interview with Rachel. He was beginning to think her stalker knew her well, that there was a reason beyond just some crazy obsession that she was doing this. Rachel couldn't know that many women personally, and of those she knew, how many of them could she have angered enough for someone to want to take revenge.

The minute he got her home, they'd begin. And he wouldn't stop questioning her until he was sure he knew everything about her.

9

RACHEL ROLLED OVER IN BED, then pushed up on her elbow and shoved her hair out of her face. A persistent ringing had drawn her out of a deep sleep. As she looked around, she realized the sound was coming from Dec's jeans, which were draped over the end of the bed.

Dec was lying beside her, his naked body sprawled across the mattress. She loved the way he slept, completely vulnerable, his body open to her touch. He was always so watchful when he was awake, but asleep, he let down his guard and she could get a sense of the man he'd be once he didn't have to protect her anymore.

They'd been sleeping together like this for three nights now, discarding the last pretenses of propriety. They'd both accepted the fact they were sharing a very intense sexual relationship and in order to continue that, it was best if they shared a bed every night.

Sleeping in his arms, his long, lean body curled against hers, gave her a wonderful sense of security. And she liked having him there to touch and to kiss when her dreams woke her up. The nightmares had eased, but Rachel still had strange dreams, fitful images of danger that often made her wake up trembling.

But he was with her now and all she needed was to

snuggle against his body to know that she was safe. She did that, throwing her arm around his waist and kissing his bicep.

Dec shifted, then opened his eyes and looked at her. A tiny smile curled the corners of his mouth and he groaned softly. "Morning."

"Your cell phone was ringing," she murmured.

He flopped back into the pillow and groaned again. "What time is it?"

"Close to nine," she said.

"Why did we sleep so late?"

"Because we didn't get to sleep until three in the morning," Rachel said.

He grinned and gave her a satisfied chuckle. "Yeah, you're right. I remember now. You were trying to convince me that your tongue was better for seduction than my hands. How did that work out? Who ended up being right?"

Rachel leaned forward and drew his nipple into her mouth, teasing at it with her tongue. "Me. You just have to admit that I know more about sex than you do."

"Book knowledge," he said. "I'm more of a hands-on kind of guy."

"Just how many women have you slept with?" she asked.

"You really want to know?" he asked.

Rachel nodded. "I don't think you'd be able to surprise me. And I probably could give it a good guess."

"I'll tell you," he said. "Just one."

"One?"

He nodded. "You. You're the only one. The rest, they

don't count because it was never the way it is with you. That was just…gratification. This is incredible, crazy, intense sex. There's a big difference." He dropped a kiss on her lips. "So how many men have you slept with?"

"One," she said with a playful smile.

"We're damn near virgins then, aren't we," Dec said.

His phone rang again and Dec cursed softly. "I should get it," he said.

"I'll get it for you," Rachel said. "I'm going to go make some coffee." She crawled over top of him then found her robe and wrapped it around her naked body. On the way to the door, she grabbed his phone out of his jeans and tossed it over to him. "One of these days, you should probably go in to your office," she said. "I don't want your employees to think I've turned you into my own personal sex slave."

"Now there's a fantasy we have to explore," Dec teased.

Rachel stopped in the bathroom to brush her teeth, then looked at herself in the mirror. She couldn't help but smile. This had become her life, here in this house, with Dec. She didn't even miss her own place and had only made quick visits home to pick up some clothes and the mail.

She reached out and set her toothbrush on the edge of the sink next to Dec's. Her make-up bag had a place on a shelf above the toilet, and her shampoo and conditioner sat on the bench in the shower stall beside Dec's.

This was what it was like to have a real relationship, one that was going somewhere. But even the growing familiarity between them hadn't entirely dispelled her doubts. What would happen once her stalker was caught? They obviously wouldn't spend their days together. Dec had a job and so did she. And they wouldn't need to live together. He'd probably want his privacy back. Would they go back to a more traditional relationship—dinners together during the week, a couple overnight stays and weekends spent together? She wouldn't be disappointed by that. But she'd grown fond of this closeness they'd developed and the intimacies that had followed.

She walked through the kitchen and opened the cupboard where Dec kept the coffee. She poured a good measure into the filter, then grabbed the pot to fill it with cold water. It was such a mundane task, Rachel thought, but satisfying. Once the coffee was done, she and Dec would relax in bed and read the morning paper. Yesterday they'd made love before getting in the shower together. Today, she wasn't sure what would happen and she liked that.

When she returned to the bedroom with the coffee and the paper, Dec was sitting up, his legs hanging over the side of the bed, a frown on his face.

"What's wrong?" she asked.

"That was my office. One of the investigators I put on your case turned up something."

"What?" she asked.

"One of your clients was arrested last year for stalking. Her name is Janice Krandall. What can you tell me about her?"

"Nothing," Rachel said, handing him his coffee.

"What?"

"Nothing. I have a strict confidentiality agreement with my clients. How did you get her name?"

"I went through the files you keep in your briefcase."

Rachel gasped, unable to believe what she was hearing. "What?"

"I knew you wouldn't tell me who they were—that you couldn't tell me—so I took it upon my—"

"Don't you dare say it," Rachel warned, grasping her coffee mug in white-knuckled hands. "You know that was completely out of bounds."

He shrugged. "It may be your job to protect their privacy, but it's my job to protect you. And I'm going to do anything I have to do. Now, tell me about this woman."

"No!" Rachel said, unable to control her anger any longer. "Do you realize what you've done? You've put my professional reputation at stake here. If my clients aren't completely assured of their privacy and my confidentiality, then they won't come to me for help."

Dec stood up and crossed the room, then grabbed her arms. "Listen closely. I don't care. If this woman is out to get you, to hell with her confidentiality."

"If you don't care about this," Rachel said, "then you can't possibly care about me. I'm a licensed counselor who is expected to follow a code of ethics. This is my career." With that, she turned and walked out of the bedroom. But once she did, she realized that she didn't have any place to go.

Cursing, she went downstairs to the small laundry room off the back hallway. There, she found a skirt and a top she'd tossed in the dryer yesterday. She stripped out of her robe and tugged the clothes on, then slipped into a pair of flip-flops.

She was out the door before she even had a chance

to think about what she was doing. But once she reached the street, Rachel realized that she really wasn't in any danger. They'd been careful to keep her location at Dec's house a secret.

Just to be sure, she headed in the opposite direction from her own house, toward a park a block and a half away. But she'd barely reached the corner, when Dec ran up behind her. He wore a pair of baggy cargo shorts and was barefoot.

"What the hell are you doing?"

"Taking a walk," she muttered. "Go home. I don't want you with me."

He reached out and grabbed her hand, but she yanked her arm away. "If you're out here, then I'm with you," he said.

"You had no right," Rachel replied, turning on him. "That crossed the line."

"It's hard to tell where the fuckin' line is," he shouted. "Where's the line going to be if you get hurt? Or if someone comes out of the dark and shoots you? Am I supposed to go back then and look for it? As far as I'm concerned, there's no line when it comes to your life."

Rachel spun around and continued walking, but he came up behind her and grabbed her around the waist, picking her up off her feet. The strength of him took her breath away and she fought against his grip.

"Let go of me!" she shouted.

"Not unless you promise to come back to the house," Dec said.

"No, I want to take a walk."

"Then you're not going anywhere."

Rachel kicked at his legs and suddenly, she hit him in exactly the right spot. He cried out in pain as his knee buckled beneath him and they both tumbled on to the soft grass of a neighbor's front lawn. She landed on top of him and Dec rolled her over, pinning her arms above her head.

"We're going home," he said.

"Let go of me."

He did as she asked, standing up beside her and rubbing his knee. "We can discuss this at home," he murmured, holding out his hand to her.

Rachel sighed, then sat up, bracing her arms behind her. "All right," she said. He grabbed her hand, helping her to her feet. Then he reached around and brushed the grass off the back of her skirt.

They walked in silence to the house. He held her hand, his fingers tangled in hers and when they reached the back door, he opened it and followed her inside. The moment the door closed behind him, he grabbed her, taking her face in his hands and kissing her. "Don't you ever get angry at me for caring about you," he murmured. "I will do whatever it takes to keep you safe."

Rachel looked up into his eyes and she saw the frustration and anger there. She couldn't blame him entirely. He probably wasn't aware of the ethical rules she was bound to follow. And after a week on the case with no decent leads, he was probably desperate enough to risk her wrath. "You'll forget her name and what you know about her, is that clear?"

He drew a deep breath and closed his eyes. Then he wrapped his arm around her neck and pulled her to him. "All right. Just don't ever run off like that again. You scared the shit out of me. I'm not sure what I'd do if something happened to you."

His hands skimmed over her body as if he needed to reassure himself that she was here and safe. Rachel felt her anger toward him slowly dissolve and before long, she returned his touch, smoothing her palms over his naked chest.

He moaned softly as she first sucked, then bit his nipple. "That's right," he murmured. "I'll take my punishment."

She reached down and grabbed his crotch and squeezed it, just hard enough to cause a little pain and he sucked in a sharp breath. "I deserved that, too. Would you like to spank me?"

Rachel stepped back and looked directly into his eyes, the blue depths twinkling with humor. "This is serious."

He reached up and smoothed his hand over her cheek. "Yes, it is," he said.

Wrapping her arms around his neck, she kissed him, tentatively at first and then with enough desire to prove to him that he was forgiven. But Dec wasn't one to leave it at that. He took control of the kiss with his tongue, sweeping Rachel into an embrace that was more than just conciliatory.

When he tugged at the hem of her shirt, Rachel lifted her arms over her head. He wasn't the only one who needed reassurance. They'd never argued like that before and she had been frightened at how angry she'd become. Dec had taken advantage and crossed the line, something that she never would have been able to forgive in another man. But forgiveness seemed to be the only thing possible now.

Dec lifted her up onto the edge of the kitchen counter and slowly teased at her nipple with his tongue. Rachel raked her hands through his tousled hair and smoothed her thumbs over his forehead, taking in all the details of his face. She'd grown so familiar with Dec that sometimes she forgot just how handsome he was.

Dec hooked his fingers in the waistband of her skirt and tugged it down, letting it drop onto the kitchen floor. Then he unbuttoned his shorts and they followed. He was already hard and ready and when he reached around and pulled her up against him, Rachel let out a soft cry of surprise.

He kissed her again, and his mouth ravaged hers, desperate to possess, to taste. Rachel drew his head back and looked into his eyes, but she could see only passion there. A thrill raced through her as she watched his desire build.

He leaned over and grabbed a bag from the counter behind her, then pulled out a box of condoms he'd purchased yesterday at the drugstore. Rachel laughed softly as she took them. "Did you leave these down here on purpose?"

"Maybe we should leave them all over the house," he said, sucking on the skin below her ear.

Rachel opened the box of condoms, handing him one and he quickly smoothed it down over his stiff shaft. He pulled her to the edge of the counter and slowly entered her, the two of them watching as he buried himself to the hilt. A tiny sigh slipped from Rachel's lips as Dec began to move.

If this was the way they settled all their arguments, then Rachel looked forward to having many more. It wasn't difficult to forgive Dec anything, especially when he made her feel like this.

DEC SLOWLY PAGED THROUGH the catalog of sex toys, stopping every so often to examine a photo in closer detail. "You know, I'm getting pretty used to these little visits to Rachel's House of Pleasure and Pain," he teased. "I never know what I'm going to find."

"There's a really nice library on campus," she said. "They have a wider selection of G-rated material."

"No, no," Dec replied. "I like the X-rated stuff. See, look at this. A life-size rubber doll for nine hundred dollars. Why would any guy need a real woman when he has a babe like this at home?" He tossed the catalog aside and picked up another. "Why do you have these? And don't tell me you're doing a study."

"I have to keep up on all the trends in sex toys," she said. "So I can talk about them on the radio. If my callers mention something I don't know about, it hurts my credibility."

"Nice," he muttered. "What about these?" He held up another catalog, open to a page of vinyl underwear. "Would you ever wear something like this?"

Rachel shrugged. "If you wanted me to wear something like that. It's only underwear. Some people find the feeling of vinyl very erotic. Like a second skin."

A long silence grew between them as Rachel continued her work. He studied her from across the room, watching the way her hair fell across her face, the way she nibbled on the end of her pen as she read. "Is there anything you can't talk about?" he finally asked.

"It's my job," Rachel replied. "It really doesn't help my listeners to be bashful. They need an honest opinion and if I act embarrassed about the conversation, then that would be a judgment on my part."

But he wasn't talking about sex and her radio show. He wanted to know exactly how she felt about him, about what had happened between them yesterday. About what had been happening between them from the moment they'd met. After their fight the previous morning, he'd felt a very subtle shift in their relationship. It was like they'd both finally acknowledged they actually *had* a relationship.

Before the fight, they were having an affair. It had been all about sex and pleasure. But the fight had proved they were two individuals with different ideas and different goals trying to find a way to live in each others' lives. If they wanted to continue to get along, then they'd have to work through a lot more conflicts.

And Dec knew there was another one coming up, starting right about now. "What time do you have to go to your group sessions?" he asked.

"We should leave here in about fifteen minutes," Rachel said. "You can drop me off. I'm sure I'll be fine. The office building is very secure."

"I'm coming in," he said.

Rachel glanced up from her desk. "If you're sitting in the waiting room when my clients get there, you're going to intimidate them."

"No, I'm coming into the group session with you."

She shook her head. "No, you can't do that. The sessions are private."

"Well then, I'll just pretend to be one of them," Dec said.

"You can't," Rachel said. "They have very specific sexual problems. You don't seem to suffer from any, beyond the fact that you think about sex twenty-four hours a day."

"Twenty-three," he said. "The other hour I spend thinking about eating."

"All right, twenty-three. They'd still spot you as a faker a mile away."

"What kind of problems do these people have?" he asked. "Why are they coming to see you? At least you can tell me that. Are they perverts or something?"

"Pervert is not a recognized name for a person with a paraphilia," Rachel said.

"You mean, these are foot people?" Dec asked. "Hey, I could be a foot person. After our night in the tub, I'm starting to develop a fondness for feet. Your feet in particular."

"They're not called 'foot people'," Rachel said. "They're foot fetishists. And I don't have a group for that."

"What are your groups?"

"I start off with my Socially Repressed Gamers. They're mostly computer guys who are approaching their thirties and have never had a girlfriend. After that, I have my sexual addicts. They're mostly divorced guys who managed to screw up their marriages by screwing around. And then I have my furries and plushies. They're a mixed group, men and women, who are sexually aroused by others in animal costumes and by stuffed animals."

"So that's the group that this Janice Krandall is in?"

"You can deduce what you must," she said. "I'm not saying a word."

"These don't sound like people who are on the edge of a major meltdown here. Why can't you just cancel until we catch the woman who's been harassing you?"

"I can't. I won't," she said. "I should be seeing them every day, but once a week is all I get. If we miss a session, then it takes another two to get back to where we were."

"I'm going to come in with you," Dec insisted. Though he knew he was pushing it, he needed to make it clear to Rachel that he wasn't going to give up so easily.

"You can't. Counselor-client privilege." Rachel drew a deep breath. "Unless—"

"What?" Dec asked.

"Unless we go in, tell them exactly who you are and why you're there and you ask permission to sit in. They'd all have to say yes before you can."

"But that won't do me any good. They'll be suspicious of me right away. No one will open up."

Rachel shrugged. "That's the deal. You can take it or leave it."

He considered the offer. At least it was a chance. "All right," Dec said. "I guess I have no choice. But if they don't let me in, then I'm going to stand outside that door until you're finished." He picked up the catalog again and stared at the cover. "Do you have dirty magazines at your other office too or do I have to bring these along?"

Rachel slammed her book shut and stood up. "Come on. We might as well get out of here now. I'm not going to get any work done with you sitting here watching me."

Dec jumped to his feet and Rachel grabbed her purse, then opened the office door. To her surprise, Simon was standing just outside, as if he'd been listening with his ear pressed against the door. Rachel cleared her throat and Dec gave the young man a wilting glare.

"I'm going over to my group sessions, Simon. I'll call in later this afternoon for my messages."

Simon gave her an uneasy smile. "I thought we were going to work on the new journal article. I have all the citations ready and I'd like to go over them with you."

"We have time on that," she said. "It's not due until September."

"But you know how busy it gets at the beginning of the school year," he said. "I think it would be best to get it out of the way now, while you have extra time."

"All right," she said. "Why don't we plan to work on it tomorrow morning. I'll come in at nine."

Dec gently took Rachel's elbow and steered her out of the office. "I don't like the way that guy looks at you," he murmured, "Your buddy Ellsworth might be right. Maybe Simon *is* in love with you."

"Don't be silly. Simon wouldn't risk his job. He's on to bigger and better things at the end of next semester."

"I just have a bad feeling about him. He's hiding something."

"Are you suspicious of everyone?" she asked.

"No, just of clingy, over-protective graduate students who think they run your life."

It was a beautiful summer day with a cool breeze blowing in off the Atlantic. They walked to Dec's car, parked near Rachel's space in the lot and he held on to her elbow, keeping a watchful eye on their surroundings.

He hadn't told Rachel about the box that had been delivered to the radio station or about the message inside. Over the past few days, she'd begun to relax again. There'd been no new contact and Dec could only hope that her stalker had found something else to occupy her time. Yet, in his head, he knew that this might just be the calm before the storm.

He'd always taken his job seriously, but this had become more than a job for him. He actually was beginning to believe he and Rachel might have a future together and Dec was willing to do everything in his power to protect that future.

It was easy to imagine himself living with Rachel, having her in his bed every night and every morning, sharing breakfast with her, calling her to chat in the middle of the day. These were such simple things, things he used to believe were unimportant. But for the guys who had a woman to love, simple things made a difference. Dec could see that now.

He opened the car door for Rachel and she slipped inside. Bending down, he tucked the hem of her skirt inside and she turned and smiled at him. And at that moment, it hit him, like running full speed into a brick wall.

"Oh, God," he murmured after he shut her door. He was in love with Rachel. He'd been so damn busy protecting her he hadn't seen what was happening to him. The revelation, though quite sudden, wasn't as disturbing as he thought it would be. He loved Rachel. What was wrong with that?

Dec tried to list all the reasons he'd always given for remaining single. He was free to date any woman who walked into his life. His time was his own. There was no one to tell him what to do or where to be. But he didn't want anyone else but Rachel and he liked spending all his time with her. And she never really told him what to do or where to be. In truth, she was happy to have time to herself.

He got into the car and fumbled with the key in the ignition. Dec glanced over at Rachel, only to find her watching him, a frown on her face.

"Are you all right?" she asked.

"Sure," he said. "Why wouldn't I be?"

"I don't know. You look a little pale." She reached out and placed a hand on his forehead. "Are you feeling sick?"

Dec shook his head. "Nope, I'm just a little hungry."

"We can stop and pick up something to eat before group. I'll be tied up from ten to two, so I'm not going to be able to catch lunch until afterwards."

"Naw, I'll be fine," he said.

"We haven't been getting a whole lot of sleep lately," she said. "I hope you're not coming down with something."

Dec chuckled. Another benefit to having Rachel in his life—someone to worry over him when he was sick. It was just getting better and better, he mused. "Are you saying I can't keep up with you?"

"Of course not," she replied. "I'm saying maybe we should try to sleep when we go to bed, instead of spending the night in other pursuits."

"Baby, as long as we're in the same room together, sleep is always going to be the last thing on my mind."

Rachel shook her head. "You're incorrigible."

No, Dec thought to himself. He was in love. And though he wasn't ready to say the words out loud, there was a certain satisfaction in knowing they were true and that someday, very soon, he would say them to Rachel.

"I VOTE WE LET HIM STAY."

Rachel smiled at Debbie. "All right. Are you sure about that?"

"No," she said. "Kyle told me to vote that way."

Rachel turned to Kyle. He held a fake fur blanket and stroked it as he glanced nervously around the room. "Did you tell Debbie how to vote?" she asked.

He shook his head. "She can never make up her mind. We'll be here all afternoon if we have to wait for her."

Rachel turned back to Debbie. "Why do you think Kyle feels that way, Debbie? Do you—"

"Can I interrupt here?"

The group turned to look at Dec, some of the members a bit taken aback by his commanding tone. Rachel sent him a warning glance. "I don't think you should," she said.

"No, I think you should let him talk," Debbie said.

Evan raised his hand, then stood up. "He's not allowed to talk until we vote for him to stay. Then he can talk."

"Will you just all get a grip!" The group turned to Daryl, who sat in his chair wearing a pair of rabbit slippers. "We have an hour. If we spend half the time talking about voting and the other half voting, then the vote is a moot point."

"My point exactly," Dec said. "Thank you. Now,

rather than discuss this, I thought we might have a show of hands. How many people want me to stay?"

"Can we have a secret vote?" Debbie asked.

"You already voted," Kyle said.

"All right," Dec interrupted. "Everyone, close your eyes. Who thinks it's all right for me to stay?"

Rachel watched as everyone slowly put their hand up. Dec nodded, then clapped his hands. "Great. Then it's settled."

"How do we know you're telling the truth?" Kyle asked.

"He's telling the truth," Rachel said. "Everyone had their hand up." This was not going well, she thought to herself. Though Dec had been invited to stay and watch her first two groups, she found him a distraction, as did many of her clients. The gamers had questioned him thoroughly and once they learned he was in naval intelligence, they wanted to hear all about it. The sex addicts were interested in hearing about his sexual conquests as a single guy. And now, her furries and plushies, the most fractured of her groups, had suddenly all voted the same. She'd never been able to get them to agree on anything before.

Rachel cleared her throat. "Now that we've got that settled, why don't we pick up from where we left off last week."

"You would be a really good tiger," Evan said, pointing to Declan.

Dec blinked in surprise. "A tiger?"

"Yeah," Debbie said. "I met a tiger once and he was so hot. He let me touch his tail. It was very erotic."

Dec frowned and Rachel could see he wasn't quite sure how to respond. "I actually think Declan would make a good bear," Rachel suggested. "He's got the dark hair and the strong jaw. And he does like to growl a lot."

"If you could dress up as any animal, what would it be?" The group turned to Janice Krandall, who'd been sitting silently to the right of Rachel. She sent Dec a hesitant smile and it was clear to Rachel that Janice had been immediately smitten with the new member of the group.

"Declan, what kind of furry would you want to be?" Rachel asked.

Dec considered the question for a long moment. "I guess I'd have to go with a horse. A stallion. A black stallion." The group stared at him and Dec glanced over at Rachel. "What? Too obvious?"

"I don't see a lot of horses as furries," Evan said. "First of all, they can't walk on two feet."

"Yes, they can," Janice said. "Those Lippizanner stallions do. And I met a horse once."

"Mr. Ed was kind of nice," Kyle piped up. "And Trigger. They'd make good furries."

The rest of the session didn't go much better. Rachel spent most of the time mediating arguments about whether certain animals could or could not be considered furries. Then, there was a very heated side discussion on the current confusion in the news media between furries and plushies. In the end, Rachel didn't accomplish anything beyond providing Dec with absolute proof that Janice Krandall couldn't possibly be capable of stalking her.

When the group finally left, Rachel sat back in her chair and watched Dec with a smug smile. "Are you satisfied?"

"I really wanted to be a stallion," he teased.

Rachel growled, then stood up. "I'm talking about Janice Krandall. You must know she couldn't be the one doing this."

Dec nodded. "Yeah, you're right. Besides, she told me she was out of town last weekend at a furry convention in Atlantic City. She couldn't have trashed your office."

"Good. So we've ruled out my clients. What's next?"

Dec frowned. "Explain to me this furry thing. They dress up in animal costumes and they mess around?"

"It's like a disguise they wear," Rachel said. "A way to hide their fears about relationships and the opposite sex. It's no different than what you might do when you meet a woman you're attracted to. You might tell a few stories, exaggerate a little, try to impress her. We all have our fears of rejection. The furries hide theirs behind a costume."

"That's a little sad," Dec said.

"It's just the way it is," Rachel replied. "Everyone has their oddities and foibles. You'd probably get turned on if I wore a French maid's outfit, right?"

Dec chuckled. "Are you saying you'd wear a French maid's outfit for me?"

"I'm saying that you relate a French maid with something sexy. These people relate a person in an animal costume with something sexy. It's not that wide a leap between the two."

Rachel stood up and walked to her desk, then put her legal pad into her briefcase. "I just think that so many people are out there trying to make a connection," she continued. "To find someone who might want to love them. And sometimes we have to make that happen however we can, even if it means dressing up in an animal suit. I don't judge any of my clients, or anyone for that matter. As long as they don't hurt someone else or themselves, then I think it's all right."

"So then why are you trying to convince them to put their suits away?" Dec asked.

"That's not what I'm trying to do. I'm trying to give them a way to see what affection and attraction can be like outside the suit. And maybe they'll find out that they can function pretty well without all that fake fur."

Dec walked to the door, then stopped Rachel before she opened it. He ran a finger along her jawline then gave her a gentle kiss. "I don't know how you do it," he murmured.

"Do what?"

"You don't make judgments," he said.

"I don't see the point," she said. "When it comes to sex and love, sometimes the journey is as important as the destination."

Rachel looked up into his eyes, losing herself for a few moments in the deep blue depths. Was he falling in love with her? Or was that just her imagination playing tricks on her? Or was it wishful thinking? He seemed genuinely fond of her, that much she could say. But Rachel still couldn't separate the man from the job. How much of what he said and did was part of his protecting her?

"I think I'd like to go home," Rachel said.

"All right. Let's go. I've got some things in the fridge we can make for lunch."

"No," Rachel said. "I want to go to my house."

Dec paused. "I don't think that's a very good idea."

"I don't care. I just want to lay down on my bed and close my eyes and pretend that my life is going to get back to normal soon. If you're good at what you do, then you can protect me there. At least for a few hours."

"All right," Dec said. "But when I say it's time to leave, then it's time to leave."

Rachel nodded, then smiled. "Thanks," she murmured.

They walked out of the downtown office building and strolled the two blocks to where Dec had parked the car. They'd driven only a few minutes when Dec cursed softly. "I think we're being followed," he murmured.

Rachel twisted to look out the back window, but he stopped her. "Don't look. Just pretend we don't see her."

"It's her?" Rachel asked.

"I'm not sure. Let me try to lose the tail and we'll see." He made a couple of crazy turns, switching lanes at the last minute and watching in the rearview mirror. Rachel held her breath, her heart slamming in her chest. Every now and then, she could see the car in the side view mirror. But then, suddenly, she watched as it turned off behind them.

"Is she gone?"

Dec nodded. "For now."

"It was probably just someone going in the same direction as we were. Now we're both getting paranoid."

"No," Dec said. "That car was definitely following us. And it fits the description of the car that Jerry gave me."

"Jerry gave you a description?"

"Of a car that he'd seen around the station," Dec said.

He shook his head. "I don't like this, Rachel. I don't think we should go to your house. It just doesn't feel right."

"Can we at least just stop there?" Rachel begged. "I need to pick up some more clothes and I forgot to grab that cookbook that I wanted."

"We'll go tonight," he said. "After things quiet down. I promise."

"All right," she said.

He stared out the front window, watching the traffic and glancing in the rearview mirror every few seconds. Rachel hated when he was forced to be the professional. The Declan Quinn she loved disappeared—the humor, the wit, the boyish charm—and was replaced by a cool, calculating stranger.

"So, how do you think I'd look in that maid's out-fit?" she asked.

A grin twitched at his mouth and after a moment, he chuckled. "Pretty damn good," he said.

10

RACHEL STOOD AT THE top of the stairs and called down to Dec. "Did you find the cookbook?"

"No," he shouted. "What's it called again?"

"*Comfort Farm Cookbook*," she said. "It has a picture of an apple pie on the front cover." She walked back into her bedroom and resumed searching her closet. She'd come to the conclusion that her wardrobe was in sad need of an update. All her clothes were entirely too conservative, not sexy. And she wanted to dress sexy now that she'd met Dec. He appreciated it and she liked his compliments.

"You are such a girl," Rachel muttered to herself.

She grabbed a flowered skirt, then turned to walk to the dresser. But she froze when she saw a woman standing in the middle of her bedroom. Slowly, the woman aimed a gun at her and Rachel felt the blood suddenly run cold in her body.

They stared at each other for a long time without speaking. And then, Rachel realized she knew the woman. "Marcy?"

"I didn't think you'd remember," Marcy said. "When Daniel introduced us at the Christmas party, you barely looked at me. I knew right away."

"Marcy, what are you doing?"

"What I should have done weeks ago, only I was too afraid. I'm not afraid anymore."

"How did you get in?" Rachel asked.

"The key. You had an extra in your desk at the university. I took it."

"Rachel!" Dec's voice echoed up the stairs. "I found it. Now come on, let's go. It's getting dark."

Marcy slowly crossed the room and held the gun up to Rachel's head. "Answer him," she said. "Answer, or I'll shoot."

"All right." Rachel called, "I'll be down in a minute. I'm just looking for that outfit that we talked about in the car." Rachel said a silent prayer that Dec's curiosity would get the better of him. She couldn't deal with this alone. He would know what to do.

"Sit down," Marcy said. "On the end of the bed."

Rachel did as she was told and Marcy sat down behind her. Closing her eyes, Rachel tried to gather her courage. If she could get Marcy talking, maybe she could convince her to put the gun down.

"How did you know about the radio station?" Rachel asked.

"You told my husband and he tells me everything about you. He's concerned about this stalker you have and of course, I pretend I'm concerned, too. But I'm really not. I'm just listening and smiling and waiting for my chance."

Marcy's voice trembled and Rachel imagined her finger twitching on the trigger of the handgun. "You don't want to do this, Marcy," she said. "There's no reason."

"I want you out of our lives," the woman shouted, anger turning her voice strident. "Ever since you came around, things have been different."

"That's not true," Rachel said.

A moment later, Dec appeared in the doorway. Rachel looked at him, sending him a silent plea. "Declan Quinn, this is Marcy Ellsworth, Daniel's wife. She just stopped by for a visit."

Marcy quickly got to her feet and stood beside Rachel, the barrel of the gun now pressed against Rachel's temple. Dec held out his hand and slowly moved forward. Though he was there to protect her, she couldn't bear the thought of him being hurt because of a situation she had caused. "Don't, Dec," she said, stopping him in his tracks. "It'll be all right."

He glanced at Marcy, then back at Rachel, sending her a warning glare. But Rachel simply smiled at him. "Marcy and I are friends," she said. "We'll find a way to work this out, won't we, Marcy?"

"The only way to work it out is to get you out of my life for good," Marcy snapped.

"How long have you felt this way?" Rachel asked. If she just kept her talking, everything would work out. That's what she had to keep telling herself or Rachel was sure she'd dissolve into hysterics.

"Forever."

"I know, it probably seems like forever to you. But it hasn't been. There was a time when things were good, wasn't there? A time when you were happy? When you and Daniel were happy?"

Marcy nodded, her lips pressed into a tight line.

"Can you remember that time now?" Rachel asked. "Because, I know you can go back there. Close your eyes and just picture it. Tell me what you see."

To Rachel's surprise, Marcy did close her eyes. The moment she did, Dec glanced over at Rachel, ready to make a move to disarm her. But Rachel slowly shook her head. "Tell me what you see," she said.

"I—I see us. We're sitting in our backyard and we're having a glass of wine. Daniel has just come home. And we have our baby girl there. She's getting so big. She walks now and she's just starting to talk. And we're watching her toddle around and laugh. And we're so happy. Everything is perfect."

"What's your baby girl's name?" Rachel asked.

"We named her Emily. Emily Elizabeth Ellsworth. Daniel said it would make a silly monogram, but when she came out, she just looked like an Emily Elizabeth, all tiny and sweet, like a little doll."

"What happened to her, Marcy? Was she too small?"

Marcy's eyes flew open and she waved the gun at Rachel. "Don't you talk about her. We never talk about her. That's why we moved here, because I couldn't stop talking about her in our old house."

"Do you think it's possible for you to be happy again? For there to be another baby?"

"Not if Daniel loves you," she said. "And as long as you're alive, he will."

"But I don't love your husband, Marcy. You do. And if you shoot me, you'll never be able to get back to that happy place. It will never happen because you'll go to jail and Daniel will be all alone."

"He loves you," Marcy shouted. "And you love him!"

"I don't," Rachel insisted.

Dec took a step forward and Marcy turned the gun on him. "She doesn't," he said.

"How do you know?"

"Because Rachel loves me, not your husband. Me. She's loved me from the moment we met. And I've loved her just the same. Marcy, she told me this and Rachel wouldn't lie to me. I swear."

Marcy's gaze darted back and forth between the two of them. "Is that true?" she asked Rachel.

Rachel looked over at Dec and smiled, hoping that it was the smile of a woman very much in love, then realizing that it couldn't be anything else. She did love Dec, so there was no reason to lie. And he'd just found a way to get through to Marcy. "Yes," she murmured. "It's true. I fell in love with him the moment we met. Actually, it was a little while after that, but it was the first night we met."

"I want a life with Rachel," Dec said. "Just like you want a life with your husband. If you shoot either one of us, then neither of us will get what we want. And that would be a real shame, don't you think?"

They stood looking at each other in silence, wondering what would happen next, Rachel trying to tell him how she felt with her eyes. And then, when they turned back to Marcy, Rachel watched her slowly lower the gun. Dec stepped forward and grabbed it from her hands before she collapsed on to the bedroom floor.

Rachel dropped to her side and soothed her as she wept, while Dec stood over them both, still watchful. "I'm going to call the police," he said.

Rachel looked up at him and shook her head. "No. No one has to know about this. I'll make sure she gets help. Sending her to jail isn't going to do anyone any good."

"Rachel, we have to turn her in."

"No!" Rachel said, gathering Marcy into her arms as the woman sobbed. "Everything will stop now. Marcy will get help and you won't say a word. Promise?"

Dec sighed. "All right. I promise."

Rachel slowly drew Marcy to her feet, then took her hands. "Come on. Let's go wash your face and comb your hair and then we'll call Daniel to come and get you."

Marcy's sobs shook her shoulders and she looked at Rachel with a tear-stained face. "I'm sorry," she said as they walked to the bathroom. "I'm sorry. I didn't mean to—don't tell Daniel what I did. I'm so sorry."

"It'll be all right," Rachel said. "He loves you. He'll understand and he'll help you."

Dec stood in the bathroom doorway, watching them both, the gun dangling from his hand. Rachel gave him a quick smile and he shook his head. "Do you have your cell phone?" she asked.

He took his out of his pocket and handed it to her. "What's your phone number, Marcy? I'll call Daniel to come and get you."

She punched in the numbers as Marcy ticked them off, then handed the phone to Dec. "Explain to him what happened and tell him to come over right away."

Dec walked back into the hallway and Rachel could hear him speaking in a low tone. She turned back to Marcy, smoothing her hand over her back. "Do you feel better now?"

The woman nodded. Rachel took her hand. "Come on, let's go downstairs. I'll make you a quick cup of tea. That will bring some color back to your cheeks."

A half hour later, Rachel stood in the foyer of her house and watched as Daniel drove away with his wife. She gripped the edge of the door, trying to keep her knees from buckling, but when Dec came up behind her and wrapped his arms around her waist, she sank back against him.

"It's over."

He rested his chin on her shoulder. "It is." His lips pressed to her cheek. "Thank God, you're safe. When I saw that gun pointed at your head, I thought I'd jump out of my skin."

"Having you there was the only way I got through that."

He cursed softly. "And I almost got you killed. I knew we shouldn't have come here. And then, I left my own gun at home. I'm sorry, Rachel. I didn't do my job."

She turned in his arms. "You did everything you needed to do."

He grabbed her face between his hand and kissed her deeply. His mouth was frantic for the taste of her and Rachel wrapped her arms around his neck and held tight, desperate herself to soothe her nerves.

Dec drew back and took her hand, then led her up the stairs to her bedroom. Rachel hesitated before stepping inside, wondering if she would ever forget what had happened there. The best way to forget would be to replace the bad memory with a good one.

She reached up and began to unbutton Dec's shirt. The rest of his clothes soon sat in a pile on the floor and she stripped off her own, then drew him along to the bed. They tumbled onto the duvet, Dec pulling her body on top of his as they fell.

He kissed her again, devouring her mouth, his hands skimming over her naked body. Dec held her so tight that Rachel wondered if he'd ever let her go. But when he finally softened his embrace, she rolled off to his side and curled up against his body.

There would be plenty of time to make love. But before they did, a question needed to be answered. Rachel just wasn't sure how to ask it. "Do you remember what you said to Marcy?"

"I said a lot of things to her," Dec replied.

"When you told her that you loved me and I loved you? And that we loved each other from the moment we met?"

"Umm-hmm."

"That was the smartest thing to say. The moment you said that, I knew we'd be safe. I don't think I ever would have thought to tell her that." She drew in a ragged breath, trying to calm her nerves. All she had to do was ask. Did he mean what he'd said or was it simply a way to pacify Marcy?

But she couldn't bring herself to verbalize the question. It was too soon and she didn't want to push him. But everything was about to change and Rachel wanted to hold on to something of what they shared.

In the end, she didn't ask. Instead, she crawled on top of Dec and seduced him, bringing him to his climax in a slow and easy way. She'd find all the answers to her questions. It would just take a little bit more time.

DEC STOOD IN THE KITCHEN of Rachel's house, peering into her refrigerator and looking for a beer. "I thought you said there was one in here," he shouted.

"Look on the bottom shelf," Rachel called from upstairs.

He did as ordered and found what he was looking for, the last bottle from a six-pack he'd brought over last week. Dec smiled as he twisted off the cap. Their lives were so intertwined already. Rachel's clothes hung in his closet, his beer stayed cold in her fridge, they'd even exchanged house keys. And sharing households was helped along by the fact that they lived only three blocks apart.

Dec leaned back against the counter and took a long sip of his beer. Life was pretty damn good, he thought to himself. And from where he stood, it would only get better.

Tonight, he and Rachel would celebrate the first month of their relationship. And though it seemed like such a short time, they'd spent more hours together than most couples who'd been dating for six months. Since he'd met Rachel, Dec had taken some well deserved vacation time. Summers were always slow for Rachel, so they'd had plenty of opportunities to be together.

In truth, Dec wanted more. Living in two houses was crazy, running back and forth for clothes and cooking supplies was starting to get to him. Tonight, he planned to ask Rachel if she might consider a more permanent living arrangement. Dec didn't care whether it was her house or his, only that they were under one roof, together.

"How do I look?" Rachel asked. She stood in the kitchen doorway, wearing a pretty celery green and white dress that left her arms and back bare. The color was perfect with her hair and eyes and complemented her pale skin.

He smiled, then crossed the room and gave her a kiss. "You look beautiful."

"When I ask you that question, I want a straight answer," Rachel scolded. "We always have to be honest with each other, all right? So if I ask if my butt looks big in this dress, I want you to tell me if it does."

"Big in comparison to what. Montana? The Space Shuttle? Baby, as far as I can see, your butt doesn't change sizes from day to day. It wasn't too big yesterday and it's not too big today."

Rachel gave him a playful slap. "You're no help."

"Then why do you keep me around?" He grabbed her around the waist and nuzzled her neck. "Is it because you love me so much?"

Rachel drew back and looked into his eyes. "Yes," she said.

At first, the meaning of her reply didn't register with Dec. And then, he slowly realized what she had said. They'd carefully avoided the sentiment, even after he'd professed his love of Rachel to Marcy Ellsworth. He'd hoped that his words that night might have initiated a discussion of their feelings, but over the past few weeks, Rachel had seemed content to go on as they had been.

Meanwhile, he'd replayed the words over and over in his head, until he came to the conclusion that he'd been telling the truth. "You love me?" he asked.

"I do," Rachel said, nodding.

"That's good," Dec replied, relief coloring his voice. "Because I love you, too."

She pushed up on her toes and kissed him, a tender kiss that they both lingered over. "I'm glad we got that straight."

"Me, too."

They kissed for a long time, as if sealing the words they'd both spoken. There was a time when Dec wondered if he'd ever say those words to a woman. He'd wondered how he'd know when the time was right. In the end, it had been so simple. He hadn't even thought before saying them, because he was speaking the absolute truth.

She nestled into his embrace and sighed. "I got a note today from Daniel. He decided to take a leave of absence from the university for the fall semester."

"What about Marcy?"

"She checked into a residential psychiatric clinic and Daniel said they're both attending daily therapy sessions. I'm sure she and Daniel will work out their problems. It must be horrible to lose a child and then to watch your marriage slip away as well."

"Well, I'm glad she's getting help. You know I wasn't too keen on keeping this from the police."

"I know," Rachel murmured. "Thank you for that."

He rubbed her back. "Are you almost ready to go?"

"No," Rachel said. She slipped out of his arms and opened the refrigerator. One by one, she removed three dishes and set them on the granite island in the middle of the kitchen.

"What's this?" he asked.

"You said we should bring a dish to dinner at your parents' house. I wasn't sure what to make, so I made three things. You know, this tradition of bringing food to a potential mates' family can be found in many different cultures. In Africa, some women are also accompanied by farm animals as well."

"Where are your animals, in the garage?"

"I'm just saying it's very important that I make a good first impression. So, which of these do you think I should bring? There's a peach cobbler, a Greek pasta salad and a really good sun-dried tomato spread for crackers. What do you think your mother needs?"

"You want me to pick one?" Dec asked. "Why don't we just bring them all?"

Rachel shook her head. "No. That would appear like I'm trying too hard."

"Trying too hard to do what?"

"To gain their approval," Rachel said.

"Baby, you don't need their approval. I love you. And if I love you, they'll love you. You come preapproved. Nothing my family could ever say would change how I feel about you." He paused and stared down at the three dishes. "Besides, you don't know how my family eats. I think we should bring them all."

She hitched her hands on her hips and considered his suggestion, then shrugged. "We'll take the hors d'oeuvres and the dessert. We can have the pasta salad for lunch tomorrow."

"Done," Dec said. "Now, let's go."

The drive down to Bonnett Harbor was one Dec had made often, but it seemed to go by so quickly with Rachel in the car to talk to. As they chatted, he couldn't help but go over in his mind how he'd tell his brothers about her. Hell, he'd been the one to issue the celibacy challenge. And he'd been the first one to break it.

He didn't care what they said. He had Rachel and that was all that mattered. She was worth whatever punishment they decided to mete out. He'd gotten what he wanted out of the challenge, a chance to know women better, a chance to find a woman worth knowing better.

As they got closer to Bonnett Harbor, he could see Rachel was getting more nervous. "You'll like my family," he said.

"So, it's your two brothers and you and your parents, right?"

"No," Dec said. "We have four older siblings, too. Two brothers, Rory and Eddie, and two sisters, Mary Grace and Jane. And then there's Ian, me and Marcus."

"Seven," Rachel said.

"We're Irish and Catholic. Big families are kind of our thing. The four oldest are married and they all have kids, so there'll be a lot of people there."

"Good," Rachel said.

When they pulled up to the Quinn house in a quiet neighborhood of Bonnett Harbor, there were children playing on the front lawn. The moment they saw Dec, they raced over to the car and hugged him. Dec introduced his nieces and nephews to Rachel, then made the two eldest carry the food into the house.

He slipped his arm around Rachel's waist and walked inside with her. He found his mother and father in the kitchen, both of them peering into a pan of barbeque sauce. "Da, Ma?"

They turned. "Declan," his mother said. "Come and taste this sauce. Your father says it needs to be sweeter."

Paddy grabbed his wife and kissed her cheek. "I said you need to be sweeter."

Emma laughed, then turned back to Declan. "So, who is this?"

Dec made the introductions and Emma immediately crossed the kitchen and held out her hand. "Rachel, I'm so glad you decided to join us." Emma looked over at her husband and smiled. "In fact, I think it's just wonderful that Declan decided to bring a friend today."

"Are Ian and Marcus here?" Dec asked.

"Oh, yes," Paddy replied. "And they'll be anxious to meet your pretty friend. You might as well get out there and make the introductions."

Dec took a deep breath. The glint in his father's eye told him that there would be hell to pay for this. Obviously he'd heard about their pact and was now taking great delight in the fact that Declan had broken it. "Well, let's go," he murmured to Rachel. "The sooner I admit defeat, the sooner I can brag about how wonderful you are."

As they walked to the backyard, Dec smiled to himself. He was proud to introduce Rachel as the woman in his life. Any man would be happy to bring her home to his family, but he'd gotten lucky. He'd been the one to win her heart. He saw Marcus and Ian standing near the back fence, tossing a football back and forth between them and Dec's two eldest nephews.

He nodded in their direction. "The guy on the right is Ian, the guy on the left is Marcus."

Rachel pointed to a nearby picnic table. "Are those your sisters?"

Dec turned and followed her gaze, then stopped short. "No." He frowned. "No, the blonde is Eden Ross." He chuckled softly. "Oh, well, this is interesting. I'm willing to bet that the other woman with the dark hair is Marisol Arantes." He groaned then raked his hand through his hair. "I should have figured this one out. God, how could I have missed this?"

"What?" Rachel asked.

He took her hand and led her out into the yard. When his brothers saw him, they stopped tossing the ball and stared. "Hey, Marky," Ian called. "I guess we're three for three."

Dec pulled Rachel against him and laughed. "You bleedin' liars. You've been shining me on all this time."

"Who's been shining who?" Marcus asked.

Dec gently rubbed Rachel's back. "Rachel Merrill, these are my brothers, Ian and Marcus. Brothers, this is Rachel. My girlfriend."

They both shook her hand then made the rest of the introductions. In truth, Dec wasn't surprised at Ian and Marisol, but Marcus and Eden Ross shocked the hell out him. When he was introduced, Eden threw her arms around him and gave him an enthusiastic hug. "Thank you for not finding me," she said.

"I'd assume you were on the boat the whole time?"

Marcus slipped his arm around her shoulders and kissed her forehead. "My own personal stowaway," he said.

Dec had never seen Marcus quite so happy. He was grinning from ear to ear. As for Ian, he'd found his match in Marisol. Like Eden, she was stunningly beautiful, but in an exotic, mysterious way.

"You're the lady with the painting," he said. "I wondered why Ian was so secretive about that."

"I guess I should thank you, too," Marisol said. "If you hadn't found that expert, I would have done something very stupid. And Ian might have had to put me in jail."

The ladies wandered off to introduce Rachel to the rest of the family while Ian, Marcus and Dec watched them from a spot near the picnic table.

"She's beautiful, Dec," Ian murmured.

"She's smart, too," Dec said. "Really smart. And sexy. I don't know how it all happened, but I'm sure as hell glad it did."

"So, what do you think?" Ian asked. "Do we give the money to the one who lasted the longest? Or do we just call it even?"

"I have an idea," Dec said. "Why don't we give the money to the one who gets married first?"

The three of them looked at each other, then laughed. "Sounds good to me," Ian said.

"I'm cool with that," Marcus added.

To Dec, it seemed as if they'd agreed pretty quickly to the challenge. He knew he had every intention of marrying Rachel. And it was obvious that his brothers felt the same way about the women they'd met.

Marcus pulled out his key chain and held out the gold medallion. "I've got it ready. All we have to do is agree."

"What is that?" Emma Quinn stepped between Ian and Marcus and took the key chain from Marcus's hand. "Where did you get that?"

"We found it when we were kids," Dec said. "In the old stable at Porter Hall."

"My mother used to wear a charm just like this around her neck. She told me that she and my father exchanged them when they were young, kind of like a promise ring." She held it up and the sunlight glinted off the gold. "It's a love charm, you know."

"A love charm?" Dec asked.

His mother nodded. "The script is Gaelic. My mother told me what it said. Let me see if I can remember. I think it was something like 'Love will find a way.'" She smiled. "That's it. Love will find a way. It's a beautiful sentiment."

The three brothers nodded. Marcus took the key chain from his mother, then slipped the charm off and pressed it into her hand. "Here," he said. "It's yours. I don't think we need it anymore."

Emma kissed Marcus on the cheek, then turned to her other two sons and did the same. "I think you boys have done well for yourselves," she said, nodding to the three women they'd brought along to family dinner. "But I can't help but wonder if the faeries have been watching out for you on this. You carry a lot of Ireland inside you and some of that is magic and some of that is luck."

"I guess our luck came all at once then," Dec said.

"I'm all right with that," Ian said.

"Me, too," said Marcus.

Dec and his brothers crossed the yard to join the rest of the family near a small wading pool that had been set up for the kids. Dec grabbed Rachel's hand and pulled her along to the house. "Come on," he said. "Let's go get something to drink."

But when they were alone in the kitchen, Dec forgot

all about the drinks. Instead, all he could think about was kissing Rachel. He kissed her because she was beautiful and sweet. He kissed her because he already knew his family loved her. He kissed her for the future they'd share and all the dreams they'd make come true.

Love had come as such a surprise, but now that he'd found it, he realized how lucky he was. Maybe his mother was right. Maybe the faeries *had* had a hand in it. However it had happened, however Dec had been chosen to be the man to love Rachel, it didn't matter.

All that really mattered was that he planned to love her until the end of forever.

* * * * *

Wait!
There are more Quinns on the way!
Don't miss...
THE LEGACY
Available next month
wherever Harlequin books are sold.
Here's a sneak peek...

1

October, 1845

MICHAEL IS GONE. Bound for Derry he is and from there will travel by ship to America. I made a brave face for his leaving, but my heart felt a terrible fear. The babe growing inside me must feel this too. Food is scarce with the potato crop ruined by blight, but Michael will find work when he lands and then will send for me. I pray for his safe journey and for the day we will see each other again.

ROSE DOYLE SAT IN THE PROTECTION of a church entrance, staring out at the cold drizzle that had turned the cobblestone streets slick. It had been raining for almost three days and the dampness had set into her bones and lungs. A cough wracked her chest and she clutched her baby closer to her body.

"It'll be fine," she murmured. "We'll find a good place to live with a warm fire and a solid roof."

Rose drew the blanket away from the baby's face, then stared down at her dirty fingers. She'd been forced to scrabble through the rubbish bins for food, joining the ranks of the poor and indigent who existed on the streets of Dublin. She knew to hide during the day and to forage at night, avoiding the authorities who might drag her off to the poor house and take her baby away from her.

Her husband was gone, dead in a raid on a tavern outside of Dublin. Jamie Fitzgerald had been a passionate patriot, a handsome young man who had put his politics before his wife and child. She'd gone into labor just an hour after the priest had told her of her husband's death and the baby had been born a month early.

"Not too early," she murmured, pressing her lips to the child's soft forehead. "You're a strong little thing, you are. You come from a long line of strong women."

Rose reached into the satchel she carried, the sum total of her life tucked inside. She withdrew the leather-bound journal and carefully flipped through the pages of tidy script. Her family hadn't had much. No pretty heirlooms to pass down to the girls, no land for the boys. But they'd had Jane Flaherty's diary, an account of the horrible years of the potato famine in the 1840s.

It had always been passed to the first-born daughter and when Rose's mother had died, her father had silently handed it to her at the wake. "You must keep the story alive now," he murmured through his tears. "This is your mother's most treasured possession and it is yours now.

It wouldn't fetch much, Rose mused. Had it been a brooch or a bracelet, she might have sold it to buy food. But then, a previous generation might have done the same and there would have been no legacy to pass along. But somehow, Rose knew that this was the way of it, that the words of Jane Flaherty had been written especially for her…to give her strength, to keep her alive when all hope seemed gone.

She opened to a favorite page and turned the book toward the light. With the diary had come an education, for Jane had taught her own daughter to read and write, and Rose's grandmother, Elizabeth, had taught Rose's mother, Bridgit. And when the time came, Rose would teach her own daughter, Mary Grace, and she would know for herself that she came from a long line of stubborn, independent and courageous women.

* * * * *

*Experience entertaining women's fiction for every
woman who has wondered "what's next?" in their lives.
Turn the page for a sneak preview of a new book from
Harlequin NEXT
WHY IS MURDER ON THE MENU, ANYWAY?
by Stevi Mittman*

*On sale December 26,
wherever books are sold.*

Design Tip of the Day

Ambience is everything. Imagine eating a foie gras at a luncheonette counter or a side of coleslaw at Le Cirque. It's not a matter of food but one of atmosphere. Remember that when planning your dining room design.

—Tips from *Teddi.com*

"**N**ow that's the kind of man you should be looking for," my mother, the self-appointed keeper of my shelf-life stamp, says. She points with her fork at a man in the corner of the Steak-Out Restaurant, a dive I've just been hired to redecorate. Making this restaurant look four-star will be hard, but not half as hard as getting through lunch without strangling the woman across the table from me. "*He* would make a good husband."

"Oh, you can tell that from across the room?" I ask, wondering how it is she can forget that when we had trouble getting rid of my last husband, she shot him. "Besides being ten minutes away from death if he actually eats all that steak, he's twenty years too old for me and—shallow woman that I am—twenty pounds too heavy. Besides, I am *so* not looking for another husband here. I'm looking to design a new image for this place, looking for some sense of ambience, some feeling, something I can build a proposal on for them."

My mother studies the man in the corner, tilting her head, the better to gauge his age, I suppose. I think she's grimacing, but with all the Botox and Restylane injected into that face, it's hard to tell. She takes another bite of her steak salad, chews slowly so that I don't miss the fact that the steak is a poor cut and tougher than it should be. "You're concentrating on the wrong kind of proposal," she says finally. "Just look at this place, Teddi. It's a dive. There are hardly any other diners. What does *that* tell you about the food?"

"That they cater to a dinner crowd and it's lunchtime," I tell her.

I don't know what I was thinking bringing her here with me. I suppose I thought it would be better than eating alone. There really are days when my common sense goes on vacation. Clearly, this is one of them. I mean, really, did I not resolve less than three weeks ago that I would not let my mother get to me anymore?

What good are New Year's resolutions, anyway?

Mario approaches the man's table and my mother studies him while they converse. Eventually Mario leaves the table with a huff, after which the diner glances up and

meets my mother's gaze. I think she's smiling at him.
That or she's got indigestion. They size each other up.

I concentrate on making sketches in my notebook
and try to ignore the fact that my mother is flirting. At
nearly seventy, she's developed an unhealthy interest in
members of the opposite sex to whom she isn't married.

According to my father, who has broken the TMI rule
and given me Too Much Information, she has no interest
in sex with him. Better, I suppose, to be clued in on what
they aren't doing in the bedroom than have to hear what
they might be doing.

"He's not so old," my mother says, noticing that I
have barely touched the Chinese chicken salad she
warned me not to get. "He's got about as many years on
you as you have on your little cop friend."

She does this to make me crazy. I know it, but it
works all the same. "Drew Scoones is not my little
'friend.' He's a detective with whom I—"

"Screwed around," my mother says. I must look
shocked, because my mother laughs at me and asks if I
think she doesn't know the "lingo."

What I thought she didn't know was that Drew and
I actually tangled in the sheets. And, since it's possible
she's just fishing, I sidestep the issue and tell her that
Drew is just a couple of years younger than me and that
I don't need reminding. I dig into my salad with
renewed vigor, determined to show my mother that
Chinese chicken salad in a steak place was not the stupid
choice it's proving to be.

After a few more minutes of my picking at the wilted
leaves on my plate, the man my mother has me nearly

engaged to pays his bill and heads past us toward the back of the restaurant. I watch my mother take in his shoes, his suit and the diamond pinkie ring that seems to be cutting off the circulation in his little finger.

"Such nice hands," she says after the man is out of sight. "Manicured." She and I both stare at my hands. I have two popped acrylics that are being held on at weird angles by bandages. My cuticles are ragged and there's marker decorating my right hand from measuring carelessly when I did a drawing for a customer.

Twenty minutes later she's disappointed that he managed to leave the restaurant without our noticing. He will join the list of the ones I let get away. I will hear about him twenty years from now when—according to my mother—my children will be grown and I will still be single, living pathetically alone with several dogs and cats.

After my ex, that sounds good to me.

The waitress tells us that our meal has been taken care of by the management and, after thanking Mario, the owner, complimenting him on the wonderful meal and assuring him that once I have redecorated his place people will be flocking here in droves (I actually use those words and ignore my mother when she rolls her eyes), my mother and I head for the restroom.

My father—unfortunately not with us today—has the patience of a saint. He got it over the years of living with my mother. She, perhaps as a result, figures he has the patience for both of them, and feels justified having none. For her, no rules apply, and a little thing like a picture of a man on the door to a public restroom is certainly no barrier to using the john. In all fairness, it does seem silly to stand and wait for the ladies' room if no one is using the men's room.

Still, it's the idea that rules don't apply to her, signs don't apply to her, conventions don't apply to her. She knocks on the door to the men's room. When no one answers she gestures to me to go in ahead . I tell her that I can certainly wait for the ladies' room to be free and she shrugs and goes in herself.

Not a minute later there is a blood curdling scream from behind the men's room door.

"Mom!" I yell. "Are you all right?"

Mario comes running over, the waitress on his heels. Two customers head our way while my mother continues to scream.

I try the door, but it is locked. I yell for her to open it and she fumbles with the knob. When she finally manages to unlock and open it, she is white behind her two streaks of blush, but she is on her feet and appears shaken but not stirred.

"What happened?" I ask her. So do Mario and the waitress and the few customers who have migrated to the back of the place.

She points toward the bathroom and I go in, thinking it serves her right for using the men's room. But I see nothing amiss.

She gestures toward the stall, and, like any self-respecting and suspicious woman, I poke the door open with one finger, expecting the worst.

What I find is worse than the worst.

The husband my mother picked out for me is sitting on the toilet. His pants are puddled around his ankles, his hands are hanging at his sides. Pinned to his chest is some sort of Health Department certificate.

Oh, and there is a large, round, bloodless bullet hole between his eyes.

Four Nassau County police officers are securing the area, waiting for the detectives and crime scene personnel to show up. They are trying, though not very hard, to comfort my mother, who in another era would be considered to be suffering from the vapors. Less tactful in the twenty-first century, I'd say she was losing it. That is, if I didn't know her better, know she was milking it for everything it was worth.

My mother loves attention. As it begins to flag, she swoons and claims to feel faint. Despite four No Smoking signs, my mother insists it's all right for her to light up because, after all, she's in shock. Not to mention that signs, as we know, don't apply to her.

When asked not to smoke, she collapses mournfully in a chair and lets her head loll to the side, all without mussing her hair.

Eventually, the detectives show up to find the four patrolmen all circled around her, debating whether to administer CPR, smelling salts or simply call the paramedics. I, however, know just what will snap her to attention.

"Detective Scoones," I say loudly. My mother parts the sea of cops.

"We have to stop meeting like this," he says lightly to me, but I can feel him checking me over with his eyes, making sure I'm all right while pretending not to care.

"What have you got in those pants?" my mother asks

him, coming to her feet and staring at his crotch accusingly. "*Baydar?* Everywhere we Bayers are, you turn up. You don't expect me to buy that this is a coincidence, I hope."

Drew tells my mother that it's nice to see her, too, and asks if it's his fault that her daughter seems to attract disasters.

Charming to be made to feel like the bearer of a plague.

He asks how I am.

"Just peachy," I tell him. "I seem to be making a habit of finding dead bodies, my mother is driving me crazy and the catering hall I booked two freakin' years ago for Dana's bat mitzvah has just been shut down by the Board of Health!"

"Glad to see your luck's finally changing," he says, giving me a quick squeeze around the shoulders before turning his attention to the patrolmen, asking what they've got, whether they've taken any statements, moved anything, all the sort of stuff you see on TV, without any of the drama. That is, if you don't count my mother's threats to faint every few minutes when she senses no one's paying attention to her.

Mario tells his waitstaff to bring everyone espresso, which I decline because I'm wired enough. Drew pulls him aside and a minute later I'm handed a cup of coffee that smells divinely of Kahlúa.

The man knows me well. Too well.

His partner, whom I've met once or twice, says he'll interview the kitchen staff. Drew asks Mario if he minds if he takes statements from the patrons first and gets to him and the waitstaff afterward.

"No, no," Mario tells him. "Do the patrons first."

Drew raises his eyebrow at me like he wants to know if I get the double entendre. I try to look bored.

"What is it with you and murder victims?" he asks me when we sit down at a table in the corner.

I search them out so that I can see you again, I almost say, but I'm afraid it will sound desperate instead of sarcastic.

My mother, lighting up and daring him with a look to tell her not to, reminds him that *she* was the one to find the body.

Drew asks what happened *this time*. My mother tells him how the man in the john was "taken" with me, couldn't take his eyes off me and blatantly flirted with both of us. To his credit, Drew doesn't laugh, but his smirk is undeniable to the trained eye. And I've had my eye trained on him for nearly a year now.

"While he was noticing you," he asks me, "did *you* notice anything about him? Was he waiting for anyone? Watching for anything?"

I tell him that he didn't appear to be waiting or watching. That he made no phone calls, was fairly intent on eating and did, indeed, flirt with my mother. This last bit Drew takes with a grain of salt, which was the way it was intended.

"And he had a short conversation with Mario," I tell him. "I think he might have been unhappy with the food, though he didn't send it back."

Drew asks what makes me think he was dissatisfied, and I tell him that the discussion seemed acrimonious and that Mario looked distressed when he left the table. Drew makes a note and says he'll look into it and asks about anyone else in the restaurant. Did I see anyone who didn't seem to belong, anyone who was watching the victim, anyone looking suspicious?

"Besides my mother?" I ask him, and Mom huffs and blows her cigarette smoke in my direction.

I tell him that there were several deliveries, the kitchen staff going in and out the back door to grab a smoke. He stops me and asks what I was doing checking out the back door of the restaurant.

Proudly—because, while he was off forgetting me, dropping by only once in a while to say hi to Jesse, my son, or drop something by for one of my daughters that he thought they might like, I was getting on with my life—I tell him that I'm decorating the place.

He looks genuinely impressed. "Commercial customers? That's great," he says. Okay, that's what he *ought* to say. What he actually says is "Whatever pays the bills."

"Howard Rosen, the famous restaurant critic, got her the job," my mother says. "You met him—the good-looking, distinguished gentleman with the *real* job, something to be proud of. I guess you've never read his reviews in *Newsday*."

Drew, without missing a beat, tells her that Howard's reviews are on the top of his list, as soon as he learns how to read.

"I only meant—" my mother starts, but both of us assure her that we know just what she meant.

"So," Drew says. "Deliveries?"

I tell him that Mario would know better than I, but that I saw vegetables come in, maybe fish and linens.

"This is the second restaurant job Howard's got her," my mother tells Drew.

"At least she's getting *something* out of the relationship," he says.

"If he were here," my mother says, ignoring the insinuation, "he'd be comforting her instead of interrogating her. He'd be making sure we're both all right after such an ordeal."

"I'm sure he would," Drew agrees, then looks me in the eyes as if he's measuring my tolerance for shock. Quietly he adds, "But then maybe he doesn't know just what strong stuff your daughter's made of."

It's the closest thing to a tender moment I can expect from Drew Scoones. My mother breaks the spell. "She gets that from me," she says.

Both Drew and I take a minute, probably to pray that's all I inherited from her.

"I'm just trying to save you some time and effort," my mother tells him. "My money's on Howard."

Drew withers her with a look and mutters something that sounds suspiciously like "fool's gold." Then he excuses himself to go back to work.

I catch his sleeve and ask if it's all right for us to leave. He says sure, he knows where we live. I say goodbye to Mario. I assure him that I will have some sketches for him in a few days, all the while hoping that this murder doesn't cancel his redecorating plans. I need the money desperately, the alternative being borrowing from my parents and being strangled by the strings.

My mother is strangely quiet all the way to her house.

She doesn't tell me what a loser Drew Scoones is—despite his good looks—and how I was obviously drooling over him. She doesn't ask me where Howard is taking me tonight or warn me not to tell my father about what happened because he will worry about us both and no doubt insist we see our respective psychiatrists.

She fidgets nervously, opening and closing her purse over and over again.

"You okay?" I ask her. After all, she's just found a dead man on the toilet and tough as she is that's got to be upsetting.

When she doesn't answer me I pull over to the side of the road.

"Mom?" She refuses to meet my eyes. "You want me to take you to see Dr. Cohen?"

She looks out the window as if she's just realized we're on Broadway in Woodmere. "Aren't we near Marvin's Jewelers?" she asks, pulling something out of her purse.

"What have you got, Mother?" I ask, prying open her fingers to find the murdered man's ring.

"It was on the sink," she says in answer to my dropped jaw. "I was going to get his name and address and have you return it to him so that he could ask you out. I thought it was a sign that the two of you were meant to be together."

"He's dead, Mom. You understand that, right?" I ask. You never can tell when my mother is fine and when she's in la-la land.

"Well, I didn't know that," she shouts at me. "Not at the time."

I ask why she didn't give it to Drew, realize that she

wouldn't give Drew the time in a clock shop and add, "...or one of the other policemen?"

"For heaven's sake," she tells me. "The man is dead, Teddi, and I took his ring. How would that look?"

Before I can tell her it looks just the way it is, she pulls out a cigarette and threatens to light it.

"I mean, really," she says, shaking her head like it's my brains that are loose. "What does he need with it now?"

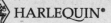

In February, expect *MORE*
from

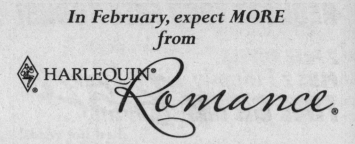

as it increases to six titles per month.

What's to come…

Rancher and Protector

Part of the

Western Weddings

miniseries

BY JUDY CHRISTENBERRY

The Boss's
Pregnancy Proposal

BY RAYE MORGAN

Don't miss February's
incredible line up of authors!

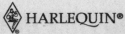

COMING NEXT MONTH

#297 BEYOND BREATHLESS Kathleen O'Reilly
The Red Choo Diaries, Bk. 1
When Manhattan trains quit and a sexy stranger offers to split the cost of a car, Jamie McNamara takes the deal. Now stuck in gridlock in a Hummer limo, she has hot-looking, hard-bodied Andrew Brooks across from her and nothing but time on her hands....

#298 LETTING LOOSE! Mara Fox
The Wrong Bed
He's buff. He's beautiful. He's taking off his clothes. And he's exactly what lawyer Tina Henderson needs. She's sure a wild night with a stripper will make her forget all about smooth attorney Tyler Walden. Only, there's more to "The Bandit" than meets the eye....

#299 UNTOUCHED Samantha Hunter
Extreme Blaze
Once Risa Remington had the uncanny ability to read minds, and a lot more.... Now she's lost her superpowers and the CIA's trust. The one thing she craves is human sexual contact. But is maverick agent Daniel MacAlister the right one to take her to bed?

#300 JACK & JILTED Cathy Yardley
Chloe Winton is one unmarried bride. Still, she asks, "Why let a perfectly good honeymoon go to waste?" So she doesn't. The private yacht that her former fiancé booked is ready and waiting. And so is its heart-stopping captain, Jack McCullough. Starry moonlit nights on the ocean make for quick bedfellows and he and Chloe are no exception, even with rocky waters ahead!

#301 RELEASE Jo Leigh
In Too Deep...
Seth Turner is a soldier without a battle. He's secreted in a safe house with gorgeous Dr. Harper Douglas, who's helping to heal his body. Talk about bedside manners... But can he fight the heated sexual attraction escalating between them?

#302 HER BOOK OF PLEASURE Marie Donovan
Rick Sokol discovers a pillow book of ancient erotic art, leading him to appraiser Megan O'Malley. The illustrated pages aren't the only thing Megan checks out, and soon she and Rick are creating a number of new positions of their own. But will their newfound intimacy survive when danger intrudes?

www.eHarlequin.com

HBCNM1206